I0764379

THE VANISHING HAND

THE VANISHING HAND

AND OTHER TALES

E. LEA WILSON

Edited and with an introduction by
Gina R. Collia

Published by Nezu Press
Queensgate House,
48 Queen Street,
Exeter, Devon,
EX4 3SR,
United Kingdom.

This edition published 2025

The Vanishing Hand first published by E. Lea Wilson
(privately printed), 1893.

ISBN-13: 978-1-917113-11-3

Cover: 19th century illustration after a painting by
Gaston Béthune (1856-1897).

In the interest of preservation, the punctuation and spelling of the original first edition text have been maintained, and the original formatting has been used wherever possible. Only minor publisher errors and spelling inconsistencies have been silently corrected.

CONTENTS

E. Lea Wilson

'Eccentric Spinster and First-Rate Storyteller'

by Gina R. Collia

Emma Lea Wilson was born in West Norwood in Surrey on 15 April 1829.[1] She was the third child and eldest daughter of Lea Wilson (1801-1846) and his wife, Mary (née Bacchus, 1803-1856).[2] Emma's maternal grandparents were George Bacchus (c.1777-1840) and his wife, Priscilla (née Ogdin, 1781-1825).[3] George was one of the founders of the renowned glassmaking company Bacchus, Green & Green, which later became George Bacchus & Sons.[4] The factory was located at the Union Glass Works in Dartmouth Street, Birmingham, alongside the Digbeth Canal. In the 1840s, the company started making Venetian-style glass paperweights, or 'letter-weights' as they were called at the time, and perfected the art of creating concentric and close-pack millefiori designs; relatively few were produced, and they are now quite rare and expensive. At the 1851 Great Exhibition, Bacchus's glassware, in particular a 'richly-cut and engraved ruby vase', was much admired by Queen Victoria and Prince Albert.[5]

Emma's father, Lea, was a silk merchant who came from a family of weavers; his family's business, the established firm of silk manufacturers Lea, Wilson and Company, was located at 124 Wood Street in Cheapside, London, and employed some 400 to 500 weavers.[6] Lea's father, Stephen Wilson (1777-1860), was responsible for introducing the first jacquard loom into England in 1820.[7] Lea's uncle, Colonel Samuel Wilson (1792-1881), was a Justice of the Peace, Harbinger to the Queen, and Lord Mayor of London in 1838.[8] Lea's cousin, Cornelius Lea Wilson (1815-1911), was a senior magistrate for Kent and a Lieutenant for the City of London; he was also an extremely wealthy man, leaving an estate worth more than £325,000 when he died (about £25 million today).[9]

Lea's mother, Sarah (1778-1864), was the daughter of Richard Lea (1747-1828), a prominent and prosperous weaver of Old Jewry in the City of London; he was elected to the Court of Assistants of the Worshipful Company of Weavers in 1786, for which he served as Renter Bailiff (1790-1791) and Upper Bailiff (1791-1791).[10] He also served as City Alderman from 1803 to 1808.[11] Richard's wife, Mary (1756-1835), came from a clerical family in Pembrokeshire; she was the daughter of Rev. Delabere Pritchett, Vicar of Carew and succentor of St. David's Cathedral.[12]

In addition to being a silk merchant, Emma's father was an ornithologist, an antiquarian, and a scholar.[13] He was elected a fellow of the Society of Antiquaries of London in March 1840, and he collected and wrote about early Bibles.[14] In 1845, he had a catalogue of his own collection privately printed: *Bibles, Testaments,*

Knight's Hill, Norwood, c. 1910.

Psalms and other Books of the Holy Scriptures in English: In the Collection of Lea Wilson Esq. F.S.A. etc. His collection included an early Wycliffe translation, originally given by Dame Anne Danvers to Syon Abbey in 1517 and now contained within the John Rylands Library at the University of Manchester.[15] Lea used this manuscript to produce his edition of *The New Testament in English translated by John Wycliffe circa MCCCIXXX*, which was published in 1848.[16] Lea was so passionate about his collection that he once offered one hundred pounds—worth about £8,000 in today's money—to anyone who would sell him a copy of the title page of the 1535 Coverdale Bible, the first complete English translation of the text; he was never able to obtain one.[17]

Lea's interest in the Bible was more than a scholarly pursuit; his family was deeply religious and a number of his relations were clergymen. Lea's younger brother Stephen (1818-1899) was vicar of St Peter's in Prestbury from 1858 to 1889 and one of the honorary canons of Chester.[18] Rev. Charles Lea Wilson (1851-1936), Lea's first cousin once removed, was vicar of St. Peter's in Old Radford, Nottingham, for thirty-three years; three of Charles's sons were also ordained. Lea's cousin Cornelius donated the land upon which St. George's in Beckenham was built, along with a stained glass window and £2,500 towards the church's building fund.[19] And his grandfather, Richard Lea, served on the first committee of the British and Foreign Bible Society, from its foundation in 1804 until 1810.[20] Sixty years later, Emma became one of the secretaries of the ladies' branch of the society in Leamington Spa, and Rev. Charles Lea Wilson's wife, Neville Juliana (née Barclay, 1851-1933), served as treasurer of the Beckenham branch.[21]

We know next to nothing of Emma's childhood, save that it was spent at her family's home on Knight's Hill Road, near St. Luke's

Lansdowne Place, Hove, c. 1915.

Church, in West Norwood, and that she grew up within a religious, financially comfortable household.[22] It is hard to imagine that a man as learned as her father would have neglected his daughter's education. Certainly, Emma inherited her father's love of books, and we do know that both of her sisters were schooled at home.[23]

Emma's father became ill at the beginning of June 1846. He was diagnosed with pulmonary gangrene and died on 27 August that year at the young age of forty-five; Emma was seventeen years old at the time.[24] Following Lea's death, his family left Norwood, and Emma, her mother, and her two sisters, Julia and Matilda, settled at 111 Lansdowne Place in Hove in Sussex.[25] Emma had three brothers; after leaving Norwood, the youngest, Percival, took up residence at 6 Bellevue, West Hill, in Hastings.[26] Arthur travelled to Trinidad in the West Indies, and George, the eldest, emigrated to Sydney, Australia, where he remained for the rest of his life.[27]

Arthur died in Trinidad in April 1853; he was only twenty-five yeas old.[28] Emma's mother died three years later, on 27 July

1856, at the age of fifty-three.[29] In April 1860, Julia married Henri Le Fer de la Motte (1832-1906) in Paris and set up home in France.[30] And in September 1862, Matilda, who was by that time living in Leamington Spa, married Edward Thomas Mason (1839-1912), a solicitor, and moved to London.[31] Following Matilda's departure, only Emma, who had left Hove and taken lodgings in Buckingham Place in neighbouring Brighton by then, and Percival remained in East Sussex, and it is likely that she moved thirty-five miles along the coast to Hastings in the early 1860s to be with her brother.[32] When Percival died of lung disease in October 1866, at the young age of thirty-four, Emma found herself living entirely alone.[33] She moved to 38 St. Mary's Terrace in Hastings, and she remained there until the end of 1873.[34] She was financially independent and lived on income from property throughout her adult life; she owned land and buildings in Norwood, including Norwood Lodge, situated on Knight's Hill Road, which she leased to Stephen William Silver, founder of the York Gate Library in Adelaide, Australia.[35]

Hastings from West Hill, c. 1915.

By the spring of 1872, Matilda's husband, Edward, then only forty-two years old, had lost his mind.[36] He was admitted to Wonford House private lunatic asylum in Exeter in Devon, and he eventually ended his days in Dr. Edward Long Fox's asylum, Brislington House, in Bristol; he died in 1912.[37] In September 1876, Matilda was diagnosed with breast cancer, and she died on 7 October 1877 at the young age of thirty-eight.[38]

With her parents and three siblings dead and her remaining brother and sister living abroad, Emma left Hastings and went to live with her maternal aunt Sarah Hopkins (née Bacchus, 1804-1896) at Norwood House on Binswood Avenue in Leamington Spa, Warwickshire.[39] Sarah had inherited Norwood House in 1874 from her brother John Ogdin Bacchus, a glassmaker like his father.[40] She was the widow of Rev. Adolphus Hopkins (1797-1855), vicar of Clent in Worcestershire from 1825 until his death.[41] Rev. Hopkins received a fair amount of public criticism during his time in Clent; beginning around 1832 and continuing for a number of years, a

The Parade, Leamington Spa, c. 1900.

The Parade, Leamington Spa, c. 1900.

parishioner called Richard Wight, who signed himself 'The Poor Man's Friend', wrote letters to the *Birmingham Argus*, complaining about the way the vicar administered his parish, in particular the way in which he distributed funds to the needy.[42] Sarah was also on the receiving end of Mr Wight's criticism; he claimed that the vicar invited only a very small number of tithe-payers to dinner on tithe-paying days, 'by his wife's special command'.[43]

Emma liked to travel, whether with company or alone. In the autumn of 1879, she visited Coatham, near Redcar in North Yorkshire, and stayed at 2 Belmont Terrace throughout the month of September.[44] The following year, she spent two months in Rhyl with Matilda's children; she and her nephews—Hugh, Herbert, and Frances—stayed at 9 Stanley Terrace from the beginning of August to the beginning of October.[45] During the autumn of 1881, Julia returned to England for a time, and the two sisters stayed at Aberdovey, on the Mid Wales coast, along with Julia's son George, who was by then a student at the nearby Jesuit college at Aberdovey

Hall in Towyn.[46] They stayed at Glanvore House, an establishment run by one Mrs Lewis.[47] And the following May, Emma visited Hastings with her aunt Sarah and stayed at 18 Robertson Terrace, a lodging house situated right on the sea front, less than a mile from her old home on St. Mary's Terrace.[48]

In the summer of 1883, Emma visited Wales again, this time with her companion Miss Hooker, from Tunbridge Wells in Kent, and she stayed there for several weeks. She began her stay at London House on Castle Road in Criccieth, a boarding house run by R. T. Prichard.[49] By the end of July, the two women had moved on to Rock House in Harlech, run by Mr William Roberts, the secretary of the Harlech Improvement Committee, and they remained there until the first week of August.[50] After leaving Rock House, they spent the remainder of August at Bronygraig, an establishment run by one Mrs Lloyd.[51]

We know little of Emma's interests or how she occupied her time, but we do know that she was religious and a charitable person.

Robertson Terrace, Hastings, c. 1910.

She gave money to various organisations, including the Birmingham and Midland Eye Hospital and the Crippled Boys' National Industrial Home in Kensington.[52] And, in addition to being one of the secretaries of the British and Foreign Bible Society, she donated money to the Church Missionary Society.[53] We also know that Emma liked to solve mathematical problems, and that she was a fluent French speaker; she was listed in the December 1888 edition of the French journal *Cosmos* as one of the readers who had sent in a solution to Kirkman's schoolgirl problem.[54] This seems to have been a problem she was very fond of; a few years later, in the 'Varieties' section of the November 1894 edition of *The Leisure Hour*, she wrote in to ask whether the solution to it could be worked out with 'a rule in some advanced arithmetic'.[55]

The Vanishing Hand: And Other Tales was published for private circulation in 1893, when Emma was sixty-four years old. It was dedicated to Emma's sister Julia, 'for whose amusement these tales were first written'. There were, of course, no newspaper notices or reviews; it was intended to be read by a specific group of people, all chosen by the author herself. The book was printed by Cowan & Co., Ltd., of Perth. Samuel Cowan was an eminent printer and publisher; he was also an historian and antiquarian—he was a member of the Society of Antiquaries of Scotland—and he wrote a number of books about Scottish history.[56]

The Vanishing Hand contains a novelette, a novella, and a short story. The title story is a criminous tale about strange goings on at Crighton Manor, the isolated home of Mrs Crighton Lewis, a 'gentle, rather eccentric old widow lady'. The tale's narrator, who is a close friend of Mrs Crighton Lewis, is an elderly spinster known to her many young friends—all '*somebody else's nieces*'—as 'Aunt Lucy'. Mrs Crighton Lewis's companion, a teenage orphan by the name of Alice Taylor, is sitting up late one night when she hears a noise at one of the doors to her room.

> 'Looking up, she saw it was partly open, and a hand was on the framework high above the lock, as if someone was steadily pushing the door against some resistance, and was about to enter.'

The hand then slowly fades away, much to Alice's horror. So, she seeks the assistance of 'Aunt Lucy', who calls in Mr. Jones, the local policeman, and with his help, and that of Lucy's *actual* nephew, Frank, a good-looking fellow and rising young barrister, the mystery is finally solved.

'A Clever Trick' concerns the lives of two young women, the stepsisters Ella and Mabel Graham. After the death of her mother, Ella's father, Robert Graham, a retired judge who has lived some years in India, returns to England and marries a comely widow he met in the train home. The new Mrs Graham has one daughter, Mabel, who, like her mother, has a tendency towards selfishness. When Mrs Graham finds herself short of money and unable to pay the debts she incurred prior to her remarriage, she alters the contents of a love letter to force a marriage between Mable and a wealthy local landowner, John Brownlow.

'An Authentic Story of a Dog' is a short tale—just four pages long in the original volume—about a stray dog, a true 'cur of low degree', who befriends the female narrator of the story in order to avoid being stoned by a young boy. He pretends to be her companion, 'just as if he had been a lady's pet all his days', which leads to the question, how does a dog who has never been a pet know how to behave like one so convincingly?

When I purchased my copy of *The Vanishing Hand*, I discovered a small note by a previous owner sandwiched between two of its pages. The note, typed on the reverse side of what looks like a distance chart from an old railway timetable or guidebook, appears to have been written around sixty years ago and contains some rather intriguing information. According to the note's author, Emma had only a handful of copies of the book printed. They had no memory of 'Miss Emma Lea-Wilson' but had been told that she was 'an eccentric spinster and first-rate storyteller'. The note goes on to say that 'there is some truth in the stories'—and notice it is *stories*, as in the plural, not just the one. In reference to 'A Clever Trick', the note explains that 'Mabel's mother doctored the address of a wealthy land-owner's love letter' in order to benefit her daughter, and this led to madness. Finally, the note's author asks that this information should not be made common knowledge: 'keep it to yourself until after I am gone.'[57]

Whoever the note's author was, they relied on a third party for information about Emma herself. However, their final request suggests that there was a more direct connection between them and the real-life Mabel or her mother; hence them not wanting to be around if the contents of the book became common knowledge. We will most likely never know who typed the mysterious note, but the suggestion that the stories were in some part true was too intriguing a possibility for me to ignore. So, with 'A Clever Trick' in mind, I looked closer at Emma's extended family, searching for some record of insanity. She did have distant relatives, two sisters, called Ella and Mabel, but they shared nothing with her characters beyond their names. I did, however, find two female relatives who may have been the inspiration for the character of Mabel.

By the time Emma moved to Leamington Spa to live with her aunt Sarah at Norwood House, the property's former owner, her uncle John Ogdin Bacchus, was dead, and it is unlikely that she ever met his wife, Eliza. John married Eliza Benson Hopkins (1804-1866)—the sister of his brother-in-law Rev. Adolphus Hopkins, already mentioned—in April 1834, but by the spring of 1851 she was a patient at The Moat House, a private lunatic asylum in Tamworth, where she remained until her death fifteen years later.[58] It was a small asylum, accommodating a handful of female patients by the time of Eliza's stay, all respectable and each having their own living quarters and attendants. The patients suffered mainly from mania, dementia, or melancholia, and they were made as comfortable as was possible.[59]

It is unlikely that Emma, only a teenager at the time, was familiar with the details of Eliza Bacchus's illness when it first became apparent. But no doubt in later life, especially during her time with her aunt Sarah, she became privy to information about her unfortunate relation's insanity. In addition to this, Emma knew the Hopkins family well and was a good friend of one of Eliza's cousins, Eliza Brush; Miss Brush was one of the few friends Emma left money to in her will.[60]

There is no way for us to know if Eliza's mother was the one who altered the contents of a love letter in an attempt to benefit her daughter. There are several ways in which the story of Mabel is different from that of Eliza. For example, unlike John Brownlow in the story, John Bacchus outlived his wife and died at the age of sixty-eight. But that typed note's writer did say that there is only 'some truth' in the stories, and, unlike Mabel, Eliza married twice. Her first husband, a gentleman by the name of Charles Ogilvy, died young; he passed away just four years after his marriage at the age of twenty-five.[61]

While looking for information about John's wife, I came across his aunt, also called Eliza Bacchus (née Arthur, 1789-1861), wife of Captain William Henry Bacchus (1782-1849) of the 18th Dragoons, 2nd Royal Surrey Militia, and 1st Provisional Battalion.[62] William founded the town of Bacchus Marsh in southern Victoria, Australia, having left England in 1837, taking his children with him but leaving his wife behind. Like Robert Graham in 'A Clever Trick', William Bacchus was a magistrate who brought his daughter up in a foreign land. And like the second Mrs Robert Graham, William's wife could be extremely manipulative and 'a very "tiger-cat" at home'.[63] Eliza was living in Greenwich in 1848, when her daughter, also called Eliza (1828-1872), who had returned to England to visit her mother, obtained a summons against her for cruelty.[64] Young Eliza, having been imprisoned by her mother, sought help by throwing notes over the garden wall, offering a financial reward to any neighbour who would contact John Ogdin Bacchus, her cousin, and tell him 'Mamma beats me worse than ever'.[65] Young Eliza was rescued, stayed in Birmingham for a time, then returned to Australia, but later in life she 'became so peculiar that she had to be put in a home'.[66] There is a memorial stained glass window dedicated to her in Holy Trinity Church in Bacchus Marsh.[67] This Eliza—Emma's first cousin once removed—appears a better fit for the character of Mabel.

Leamington viewed from Newbold Comyn, c. 1829.

Emma appears to have created the background stories of her characters in 'A Clever Trick' by piecing together events from her various relatives' lives, altering details here and there without obscuring the original histories, which would have been instantly recognisable to members of her own family; as would the names of her characters, which seem to have been taken from various Leamington Spa locations or inhabitants. Newbould Grange, the home of John Brownlow, was most likely named after Newbold Comyn manor house or any of the streets which also take its name. Laura Greville shares her family name with a street in the town and the earls of neighbouring Warwick. Robert Graham shares his name with the well-known Leamington Spa photographer Robert L. Graham, who had a studio on The Parade when Emma lived there. And whilst there was no old, established chemist shop called

Messrs. Griffin & Sons in Leamington Spa, there were millers by that name in Warwick.[68]

Looking now at 'The Vanishing Hand', this tale can be dated to 1889 or 1890, as Emma included a real-world tragedy in her story: the Ring Theatre fire in Vienna which took place in 1881. In the story, Alice's parents both died in that fire when she was around ten years old, and she is eighteen years old when she becomes Mrs Crighton Lewis's companion. The beginning of the story is set in Ailsbury in Greenshire, which is surely a thinly-disguised reference to Aylesbury in Buckinghamshire; the action then shifts to the peaceful village of Crighton. Interestingly, whilst there was no Mrs Crighton Lewis in existence when Emma was writing about her, there had been a Mr & Mrs Henry Creighton Lewis, and, as with the elderly widow in the story, they had lost a child in infancy. Henry ran the Bell Hotel in Market Square in Aylesbury, and his daughter's wedding was reported in the *Lady's Pictorial* and the *Gentlewoman* in 1891.[69] It is possible, considering the timing of the event, that Emma saw the wedding notices and took Henry's family name and the location of his home to use in her story. Alternatively, given his occupation and Emma's love of travelling about, she may have stayed at his hotel, or at least visited it at some point during her excursions.

The character of Frank Wagram may have been based on Cecil Frederick Joseph Jennings, Emma's cousin, who was an up-and-coming young solicitor at the time the story is set; he later became Under-Sheriff of the City of London. He and Emma were very close, and she appointed him as one of the executors of her will.[70] And I cannot help but wonder if Emma, who does appear to have been partial to a little intrigue, inserted something of herself into the story in the form of 'Aunt Lucy'.

As to Emma's decision to write about the theft of valuable silverware, she may have been inspired by events which took place at and near the home of Cornelius Lea Wilson, already mentioned, in the Kentish village of Beckenham in the spring of 1890. In the early hours of 19 March, a burglar attempted to gain entry to Cornelius's home, The Cedars, but found that, as the property's window sashes were fitted with screws to restrict their opening, he could not climb inside the house.[71] He then made his way across fields to the secluded rectory of Rev. Henry Arnott and, prising open the study window, proceeded to steal various silver items, including a cherished family heirloom, worth in excess of four thousand pounds in today's money.[72] Apparently, the burglar 'went about his work in a very cool and determined manner', going so far as to light a candle and keep it burning for about an hour, and all the while the rector slept soundly in his bed upstairs.[73] Local newspapers reported that the police were left with 'no clue'.[74]

There had been a spate of burglaries in Beckenham and its vicinity around the time that the rector's silverware was stolen, and a month or so after the burglary at the rectory, Detective Inspector Fox and Inspector Bunting of P. Division at Lewisham arrested three men who they believed were responsible for most if not all of the thefts.[75] Interestingly, after their arrest they were taken to Beckenham police station to be charged, and the senior magistrate they appeared before was none other than Cornelius Lea Wilson.[76] The men were tried at Maidstone Assizes in July, and two of them—Henry Scott, a well-known burglar from East Dulwich, and Henry Smith, a hammerman from Walworth—were sentenced to twelve years' imprisonment.[77] The third man, Henry Clark, a labourer from Camberwell, was sent to prison for five years.[78] The burglaries had created quite a stir, and, after sentencing Scott and

Smith, the judge remarked that 'great credit was due to Inspector Fox and the other officers, for the diligence and intelligence displayed by them in the case, by which the neighbourhood had been rid of two of the most notorious rascals in existence.'[79]

For obvious reasons, I found nothing to prove or disprove the contents of 'An Authentic Story of a Dog', but we should probably take it as given that Emma did encounter such a 'cur of low degree' at some point and act as his protector. Presumably someone familiar with Victorian Brighton, Hove, or Hastings would have been able to identify the seaside location chosen for her tale.

In the same year that Emma published *The Vanishing Hand*, advertisements for the *Church of Ireland Penny Magazine* indicated that a 'Serial Story' by E. Lea Wilson was included in the March edition of the journal.[80] I have been unable to locate a copy of this edition; in fact, I have been unable to locate *any* copy of this magazine. Advertisements for it appeared for just two years, from February 1842 to February 1894, and it seems to have disappeared as quickly as it appeared.

The Vanishing Hand would appear to be Emma's only surviving published work. However, it is obvious that she was, as the writer of that note informed us, 'a first-rate storyteller'. The stories are not the work of a one-time amateur, and it is likely that she regularly entertained her family and friends with similar tales throughout her life. Perhaps she told her tales at the fireside; perhaps she enclosed them with letters to her sister in France. Unfortunately, we shall never know. There is no copy of *The Vanishing Hand* in any public library; if it were not for a few brief references to it here and there, and the fact that a copy sits on my bookshelf, we would not know of *this* book's existence, and I would not be writing about it now. There could be other titles out there that Emma published for the entertainment of those close to her; she certainly had the ability and finances to produce more. So, we can but wait… and hope.

Emma's aunt Sarah died on 8 October 1896, leaving £3,000 to her niece, plus a legacy upon trust for her of £1200.[81] Following Sarah's death, Emma moved from Norwood House to 29 Clarendon Street, where she remained for the final eighteen months of her life.[82] She had developed paralysis on one side of her body at the beginning of 1896, most likely as the result of a stroke, and she died as a consequence of this and exhaustion on 21 February 1898; she was sixty-eight years old.[83]

Notes

1 Norwood was in the historic county of Surrey; it is now in the South London borough of Lambeth. *England & Wales, Non-Conformist and Non-Parochial Registers, 1567-1936*, and *The Observer*, 26 April 1829, p. 4.

2 Lea Wilson's dates: *England & Wales, Non-Conformist and Non-Parochial Registers, 1567-1936*, and *London, England, Church of England Deaths and Burials, 1813-2003.* Mary Wilson's dates: *England & Wales, Non-Conformist and Non-Parochial Registers, 1567-1936*, and *Brighton Gazette*, 7 August 1856, p. 5.

3 George's dates: *Worcestershire, England, Church of England Deaths and Burials, 1813-1997.* Priscilla's dates: *England & Wales, Non-Conformist and Non-Parochial Registers, 1567-1936*, and *London, England, Church of England Deaths and Burials, 1813-2003.*

4 Bacchus, Green & Green was founded in 1818. It became George Bacchus & Co. in 1833, and following George Bacchus's death in 1840 it was renamed George Bacchus & Sons. The name was changed to Bacchus & Sons in 1858. See, Lawrence Selman, *The Art of the Paperweight*, Paperweight Press, 1988, p. 48.

5 *Coventry Herald*, 18 July 1851, p. 3.

6 *London, England, City Directories, 1736-1943*, and Alfred Plummer, *The London Weavers' Company, 1600-1970.* London: Routledge & Kegan Paul, 1972, p. 334.

7 Clinton G. Gilroy, *The Art of Weaving.* New York: George D. Baldwin, 1844, p. 192. Stephen Wilson's dates: *England & Wales, Non-Conformist and Non-Parochial Registers, 1567-1936*, and *England & Wales, National Probate Calendar (Index of Wills and Administrations), 1858-1995.*

8 The Harbinger to the Queen was an 'agent in advance', responsible for going ahead of the queen and securing suitable lodgings, etc., when she travelled.

9 *England & Wales, National Probate Calendar (Index of Wills and Administrations), 1858-1995.*

10 Sarah Wilson's dates: *England, Select Births and Christenings, 1538-1975*, and *UK, Burial and Cremation Index, 1576-2014*. Information about Richard Lea: Plummer, op. cit., p. 340. The Worshipful Company of Weavers is the oldest of London's livery companies. Richard Lea's dates: *England, Select Births and Christenings, 1538-1975*, and *London Evening Standard*, 8 December 1828, p. 4.

11 Plummer, op. cit., p. 340.

12 Mary Lea's dates: *England, Select Births and Christenings, 1538-1975*, and *London, England, Church of England Deaths and Burials, 1813-2003.*

13 *A Prospectus of the Works on Ornithology, etc., by John Gould, F.R.S.; With a List of Subscribers to, or Possessors of the Works*, 1868, p. 26.

14 *A Copy of the Royal Charter and Statutes of the Society of Antiquaries of London.* London, 1837, p. 19.

15 *Bibles, Testaments, Psalms and other Books of the Holy Scriptures in English: In the Collection of Lea Wilson Esq. F.S.A. etc.* London: William Pickering, 1845, p. 137. John Rylands Library Accession no. R4995.

16 *The New Testament in English translated by John Wycliffe circa MCCCLXXX: now first printed from a contemporary manuscript formerly in the monastery of Sion Middlesex late in the collection of Lea Wilson F.S.A.* London: William Pickering, 1848.

17 *The Athenaeum*, 11 August 1877, p. 181.

18 *Chester Chronicle, and Cheshire and North Wales General Advertiser*, 8 April 1899, p. 8.

19 *The British Architect and Northern Engineer*, 26 May 1876, p. 277. £2,500 would be worth about £165,000 in today's money.

20 William Canton, *A History of the British and Foreign Bible Society*. London: John Murray, volume II, 1904, p. 462.

21 *The Seventy-Fourth Report of the British and Foreign Bible Society; MDCCCLXXVIII. With an Appendix and a List of Subscribers and Benefactors*, 1878, p. 25.

22 *1841 England Census.*

23 *1851 England Census.*

24 Death certificate for Lea Wilson, district of Norwood in the county of Surrey, 1846.

25 *England & Wales, National Probate Calendar (Index of Wills and Administrations), 1858-1995.*

26 *1866 Post Office Directory of Sussex, and South London Journal*, 3 November 1866, p. 4.

27 Arthur: *England & Wales, National Probate Calendar (Index of Wills and Administrations), 1858-1995.* George: *Sydney Morning Herald*, 7 February 1856, p. 4, and *Australia Death Index, 1787-1985.*

28 *England & Wales, National Probate Calendar (Index of Wills and Administrations), 1858-1995.*

29 *Brighton Gazette*, 7 August 1856, p. 5.

30 *Paris, France, Births, Marriages, and Deaths, 1555-1929.*

31 Edward's dates: *London, England, Church of England Births and Baptisms, 1813-1924*, and his death certificate, which states that he died in Brislington House, a private lunatic asylum established by Dr. Edward Long Fox, in 1912. Matilda's marriage: *Warwickshire, England, Church of England Marriages and Banns, 1754-1910.*

32 *England & Wales, National Probate Calendar (Index of Wills and Administrations), 1858-1995.* Emma's address was listed in the letters of administration of her brother Arthur.

33 Death certificate for Percival Lea Wilson, and *1866 Post Office Directory of Sussex, and South London Journal*, 3 November 1866, p. 4.

34 *1871 England Census.* She was listed as a freeholder and copyholder. Also, *Hastings & St. Leonards Advertiser*, 11 December 1873, p. 10.

35 Emma's will for details of her property ownership and her lease to Stephen William Silver. Address of property, see *UK, Poll Books and Electoral Registers, 1538-1893.* Address given as Crown Hill, which was the name of the road in the 1860s.

36 See Mason v Jennings, cause no. 1872 M47, The National Archives, Kew.

37 *Exeter and Plymouth Gazette*, 12 May 1885, p. 1. A death notice for Matilda, published eight years after her death, includes the fact that Edward was a resident at Wonford House when she died. His final address, Brislington House, was included in the register of deaths.

38 Death certificate for Matilda Lea Wilson, and *England & Wales, National Probate Calendar (Index of Wills and Administrations), 1858-1995.*

39 Emma's name was included in *The Seventy-Fourth Report of the British and Foreign Bible Society; MDCCCLXXVIII. With an Appendix and a List of Subscribers and Benefactors*, 1878, p. 25. She was listed as a secretary of the Leamington Spa branch for the year 1878, so she must have moved to her aunt's house on Binswood Avenue before the spring of that year. Emma's address: *1881 England Census*. Sarah's dates: *England & Wales, Non-Conformist and Non-Parochial Registers, 1567-1936*, and *England & Wales, National Probate Calendar (Index of Wills and Administrations), 1858-1995.*

40 *England & Wales, National Probate Calendar (Index of Wills and Administrations), 1858-1995.*

41 *England, Select Births and Christenings, 1538-1975*, and *England and Wales, Prerogative Court of Canterbury Wills, 1384-1858.*

42 John Amphlett, *A Short History of Clent.* London: Parker and Co., 1890, pp. 171-172.

43 Ibid., p. 172.

44 *Redcar and Saltburn-by-the-Sea Gazette*, 5 September 1879, p. 4, and 19 September 1879, p. 4.

45 *Rhyl Record and Advertiser*, 7 August 1880, p. 2, and 2 October 1880, p. 4.

46 *Aberystwyth Observer*, 10 September 1881, p. 8, and *1881 Wales Census.*

47 *Aberystwyth Observer*, 10 September 1881, p. 8.

48 *Hastings and St. Leonards News*, 12 May 1882, p. 5.

49 *The Cambrian News and Merionethshire Standard*, 20 July 1883, p. 2.

50 Mr Roberts: *Atherstone, Nuneaton and Warwickshire Times*, 19 June 1880, p. 3. Emma's stay at Rock House: *The Cambrian News and Merionethshire Standard*, 20 July 1883, p. 2, and 3 August 1883, p. 2.

51 *The Cambrian News and Merionethshire Standard*, 10 August 1883, p. 6, and 24 August 1883, p. 6.

52 *The Times*, 25 October 1893, p. 2, and *Birmingham Daily Post*, 19 September 1890, p. 6, and 18 September 1891, p. 6.

53 *The Church Missionary Gleaner*, February 1889, p. 32.

54 *Le Cosmos: Revue des Sciences et de Leur Applications*, 8 December 1888, p. 52. A problem in combinatorics proposed by Thomas Penyngton Kirkman in 1850. The problem, explained by Emma in The Leisure Hour, is: 'In a fashionable boarding school fifteen young ladies are to walk out every day for seven days, three in a row; but so arranged that during the seven days no two of the fifteen are to walk together twice.'

55 *The Leisure Hour*, November 1894, p. 67.

56 Scottish Printing Archival Trust, *A Reputation for Excellence: A History of the Dundee and Perth Printing Industries*. Edinburgh: Merchiston Publishing, 1996.

57 When considering the accuracy of the note's contents, it must be remembered that nowhere in the text of her book is Emma's Christian name given; neither is her marital status. Both were known by the note's author. A stranger purchasing the book from a secondhand bookseller would not have had this information, and the Internet did not exist in the 1960s. Whoever typed that note did not know Emma, but he or she certainly knew people who did.

58 *UK, Lunacy Patients Admission Registers, 1846-1921.*

59 *Reports from Commissioners: Seventeen Volumes*, vol. 18. House of Commons report, 1844, p. 135.

60 To Eliza Brush of 2 St Winifred's, Great Malvern, Emma left the sum of £100 (worth about £8,000 in today's money).

61 *England & Wales, Prerogative Court of Canterbury Wills, 1384-1858.*

62 National Archives, Kew, catalogue ref. WO 25/750/42.

63 From 'A Clever Trick', see p. 46.

64 *West Kent Guardian*, 12 August 1848, p. 5.

65 Ibid.

66 *Bacchus Marsh Express*, 21 April 1934, p. 4.

67 *Bacchus Marsh Express*, 24 October 1936, p. 4.

68 *Leamington, Warwick, Kenilworth & District Daily Circular*, 18 September 1899, p. 3.

69 Reports of the wedding refer to the bride's father as Creighton Lewis, solicitor. Though he had started out as a solicitor's clerk, he became an inn-keeper and registrar of births, deaths and marriages, see *London, England, Church of England Marriages and Banns, 1754-1940*, and *England & Wales, National Probate Calendar (Index of Wills and Administrations), 1858-1995*. It was not unusual for people to upgrade their father's profession when getting married.

70 Arthur Charles Fox-Davies, *Armorial Families: A Directory of Gentlemen of Coat-Armour*. London: Hurst & Blackett, 1929, p. 1052.

71 *Beckenham Journal*, 22 March 1890, p. 7.

72 Ibid., and *Lloyd's Weekly Newspaper*, 23 March 1890, p. 5.

73 *Croydon Advertiser and East Surrey Reporter*, 22 March 1890, p. 8.

74 Ibid.

75 *Beckenham Journal*, 26 April 1890, p. 6.

76 Ibid.

77 *Beckenham Journal*, 19 July 1890, p. 5.

78 *Bromley & District Times*, 18 July 1890, p. 5.

79 Ibid.

80 *Cork Constitution*, 7 March 1893, p. 4. Advertisements for the magazine appeared from February 1842 to February 1894, stating that it was available from the Religious Tract & Book Society, 35 Grand Parade, Cork, and that all orders should be addressed to the manager, Thomas Morgan. It seems that the *Cork Constitution* was the only paper to carry the advertisements. Though the magazine appears to have been marketed as a monthly, it seems that only a few editions were actually published.

81 The will of Sarah Hopkins of Norwood House, Leamington, dated 16 October 1895, and *England & Wales, National Calendar (Index of Wills and Administrations), 1858-1995*.

82 *Spennell's enterprise Almanac and Annual Advertiser for 1897 with Directory of Leamington, Warwick, Kenilworth, Stratford-on-Avon and the District*, and Emma's death certificate, issued in the sub-district of Leamington in the country of Warwick.

83 Death certificate; cause of death certified by Dr Thomas W. Thursfield, who was also the Mayor of Leamington Spa at the time.

THE VANISHING HAND

THE VANISHING HAND

CHAPTER I

"AUNT Lucy, did you ever see a ghost?"

This sudden question came from a girl sitting near the window of my library. She was at the charming age when early girlhood is entering the graver stage of womanhood. No longer "a young thoughtless thing," joyful as a butterfly on a June morning, but quieter and somewhat more serious in her mind and manners than the brief nineteen summers which had as yet passed over her head would quite warrant.

"No," I answered measuredly, "I am quite sure that I never did see a ghost."

There followed a pause. The words took my thoughts back some thirty years. There were some sharp salient way-marks in my life; never would they be effaced; there were dulled remembrances of what was once well-nigh agony—of a whole life's course changed by a cruel practical joke.

"Aunt Lucy, did you ever *think* you saw a ghost?"

There was something in her tone which made me look up, and instead of the half-jesting, half-ridiculing expression of face I expected to see, there was a look of such earnest anxiety in her large, dark eyes, that instead of the "Don't talk nonsense" which was on my lips, I merely said quietly, "I do not think a ghost, as you call it, is impossible, but I do think authentic cases are exceedingly rare, and I am inclined to believe that even those so-called authentic cases might frequently have been traced either to simple material causes, or to a more complex physical origin. Certainly we are near, very near to the borders of the supernatural world, and I should not dare to deny the possibility of such things, even though the why and the wherefore and the how escape the limits of our intelligence; but, my dear child, is it a psychical discussion you are proposing to me, or—what has happened to you? Why do you ask me the question?"

Alice suddenly rose, crossed over to where I was sitting, and placing herself on a footstool quite close to me, put her hand into mine, and said, "Oh, dear Aunt Lucy, don't laugh at me, but I do, indeed, think I saw a ghost last night!"

The girl's words startled me. Alice, whose life history had been so full of sorrow, anxiety, and difficulty, all borne so bravely, and with such practical good sense; Alice, who could not possibly be called romantic, who when speaking of novels said that she had no patience to finish them! *She* thinking seriously that she had seen a ghost!

I replied, however, calmly, "Tell me all about it, exactly as it happened; perhaps we shall find the clue if we put our heads together. What was it that you saw?" I did not, I felt I could not say, "all you *think* you saw;" the grave, anxious, awed expression of the young face imposed a check on the words as they rose to my lips.

We were very peaceful there in my library, the soft morning sunshine streaming into the room, tempered by the partial shade of the old-fashioned green blinds. It was about nine o'clock. Alice frequently came to me to breakfast, for Mrs. Crighton Lewis, the gentle, rather eccentric old widow lady with whom Alice Taylor lived as reader and companion in an old manor house about a mile from my cottage, never required her to be with her before twelve o'clock. Then in the quiet morning hours I heard what I will now tell as a story, varying the conversational tone I have hitherto adopted.

Alice was an orphan. Her father and mother had simultaneously met their deaths in the terrible fire in the Ring Theatre in Vienna.[1] She was then not much more than ten years old. Her father's only brother, Mr. Charles Taylor, took her to live in his house at Ailsbury in Greenshire. He was a cold, stern man, and was rendered colder and sterner still by the temper of his wife, and by the habits of inebriation which she had unhappily contracted. Her very life had been soured by the fact that she had no children.

Poor little Alice soon learnt that no kindness was to be expected from her aunt. She was not actually ill-treated, but she received exactly what was absolutely necessary in food, clothing, and instruction, and that was all. Naturally quick, she contrived to make the most of the few months of second-rate teaching she received, and as she grew older, fortunately for her, she discovered a large forgotten box in the loft, which contained the school books which had once belonged to a younger brother of her aunt's. Many comparatively happy hours did she spend, studying according to a plan she had found among the books. Geography, history, grammar, etc., so many times a week, and so on. Thanks to her perseverance and indefatigable industry, she was far from ignorant.

When Mr. Charles Taylor died she was about eighteen. A few days after the funeral her aunt said to her, "You are aware you have nothing; you must not expect me to keep you. You must get your own living."

Alice replied, "Get me a situation and I will gladly do so." She ventured to ask what kind of place her aunt thought her fitted for.

---

[1] The Ring Theater fire was a real event that took place at Schottenring 7 in Vienna on 8 December 1881. Fire broke out on stage shortly before a performance of *Les Contes d'Hoffmann.* The building was gutted within a few hours, and at least 384 people lost their lives.

"Fitted for, indeed," was the harsh reply, "I shall place you with anyone who will take you, beggar that you are!"

Utterly inexperienced though she was, Alice's mind was filled with a vague anxiety. Still the prospect of getting away from her aunt was a relief, and youth is ever apt to believe that any change must be for the better. In the evening of the day when the foregoing conversation occurred, Alice strolled down the garden, and opening the gate, walked a few paces along the hight road. As she turned to re-enter the garden she perceived the clergyman of the parish approaching.

He had always been kind to her on the rare occasions when he had spoken to her, and there had always been that in his manner which made her feel instinctively, "He would be kinder still to me if he could!" When he saw Alice he quickened his pace, and naturally, she walked to meet him. After inquiring after her health, he abruptly asked her whether she was going to continue living with her aunt. Alice simply related to him the conversation of the morning.

He reflected in silence a few moments, and then said: "You are no longer a child, and will, I am sure, be sensible and prudent in any case, but promise me this: as soon as you have a place, I mean, as soon as you have left your aunt's care, write to me, and tell me exactly what she has done with you and for you. Notice everything, the name of the street you may lodge in, the names of the persons she takes you to; tell me all, even trifles. Write again and again if you are in difficulty and anxiety. Remember, I am most anxious to be your friend. Do not leave off writing until you know from myself that I know where and with whom you are; letters may miscarry, you know; only, always try to post your letters yourself." A sudden thought struck him, he took a pocket-book from his pocket, and, putting several stamped envelopes and a small sum of money into her hand, he went on: "Take these, and whatever happens to you, let me know it. No thanks, no thanks; let me treat you for once as if you were my own little girl . . . . I trust Providence has good in store for you, but it may be the reverse." Alice gratefully promised to obey the kind clergyman. "Try and come to say good-bye to us all at the vicarage," he said; "Mrs. Griffith is always pleased to see you, but if you do not come, we shall know that you have been prevented. Now, run in, and do not forget your promise." He shook hands kindly with her, and as he continued his way, he murmured to himself: "Poor child, poor child! that aunt of hers is a cruel, bad woman, or I am much mistaken! I dared not say more for fear of frightening the poor little thing. May Providence guard and watch over her!"

The good man's prayer was heard, and the evils which he vaguely dreaded were happily averted from her path.

The next day her aunt conducted her to an agency in London. The agent told her of a place in a shoemaker's family as nurse-girl, and binder in her odd hours.

As Mrs. Taylor was desirous of accepting the position for her niece, the man offered to send for the shoemaker's wife, who lived a short distance off, and arrange matters then and there. Mrs. Taylor said she would leave Alice to wait in the office, and would herself return in an hour. Giving the poor girl a penny roll, she went to get a comfortable repast for herself. Hardly was she out of sight, when most providentially an eccentric old lady named Mrs. Crighton Lewis walked into the office. The old lady had scarcely begun to explain the business which brought her there, when she was seized with a violent bleeding of the nose. Alice sprang forward and waited upon her with quiet, gentle care. When the accident had terminated, the lady spoke to her, and inquired what she was doing there. The agent replied that the young person was about to be placed as I said before.

Mrs. Crighton Lewis looked at the wistful brown eyes and said: "Can you read aloud nicely, child?"

"I think so," was the reply, given in a musical, ladylike voice.

"Would you like to come and live with me? I'll be kind to you, girl."

"Indeed, I should like it," replied Alice.

Fortunately, at that moment a message from the shoemaker arrived, to the effect that he had decided to take a paying apprentice, instead of a girl who would be an expense to him.

When Alice's aunt returned, the agent informed her of the refusal of the shoemaker to take Alice, and of Mrs. Crighton Lewis' offer. Mrs. Taylor, who was delighted to be rid of her niece on any terms, immediately closed with the proposal, in fact, stipulated for food and clothing, and that was all. Mrs. Crighton Lewis saw that the woman was the worse for what she had imbibed with her luncheon, hastily concluded the affair, and took the poor child away with her in her carriage at once, her small box taking very little room, so little that even the coachman forgot to grumble. Mrs. Taylor never even asked where Alice was being taken to . . . . She was off her hands, and that was all the hard-hearted woman cared to know.

Mrs. Crighton Lewis wrote at once to Mr. Griffith, the vicar of Ailsbury. His answer was not long in coming. It was long, and it was confidential, for it so happened that he was no stranger to her, nor for that matter was he a stranger to me either, though many many years had passed since I had either seen him or heard from him. The first result of his letter was the fact that Mrs. Crighton Lewis called Alice to her, and after kissing her affectionately on the cheek, the first kiss the child had received for many a long year, said to her:

"My child, you know you are to be my little companion and friend; I shall allow you £10 a quarter for your dress and other expenses. Nurse (my old housekeeper) will give you the necessary advice and help with your dress. I wish you to be quietly but nicely dressed. You can, when we are in London, take some lessons in drawing, or other things if you are so inclined, in the hours in which I leave you free. It shall not be my fault if you are unhappy in my very quiet life."

Alice was touched by her kindness and by what seemed to her, her munificence, and resolved to do her utmost to please the old lady to whose care Providence had confided her. She was a gentle, ladylike girl, somewhat too timid perhaps, or rather unused to society, but her entire absence of self-consciousness, and her sweet, obliging disposition, completely excluded anything like awkwardness from her manners. Unused to kindness, her nature expanded under its influence like flowers in the sunlight, and everyone, from Mrs. Crighton Lewis down to the smallest stable-boy with whom she came in contact, was drawn to her by the charm of her gentle, obliging ways.

I heard from Mrs. Crighton Lewis the details of the manner in which Alice had become her companion. I was the confidante of her plans concerning her, and in my now somewhat lonely life I was delighted to receive this sweet girl into my heart, and after carefully watching her at first, and finding her to be as good and pure as her dear bright face was pretty and winning, I thoroughly enjoyed directing her reading, and supplying her with books which enabled her to reduce to order the really important, but somewhat crude mass of knowledge she had acquired from her steady work by herself in that draughty loft in her uncle's house at Ailsbury. I encouraged her to come and see me often, as I said before, and very soon the name "Aunt Lucy," by which I was known by many young friends, *somebody else's nieces*, came quite familiarly from her lips. I look back on the morning with Alice before the events I am about to relate as some of the pleasantest in my later years.

The manor house, Crighton Manor as it was called, was a large, rambling building. The situation was very lonely, surrounded as it was by old-fashioned shrubberies and gardens. It stood on a hill, and the pine woods belonging to the property came almost up to the house on three sides of it, and sloped down, a very sea of green and brown ferny waves, as far as anyone would care to walk in an hour. The gardens were closed in by high walls, and the carriage drive was completely under the over-arching trees on either side of it.

Mrs. Crighton Lewis had herself chosen a very nice bedroom for Alice. A large, handsome room it was, opening on to the wide landing which ran across the east side of the manor house. Two windows opened on the pine trees which, beginning on that side, belted the house round to the north and west. The door was opposite to the windows. A wide stone coping went from end to end right under the windows; it was covered in many places by ivy and Virginia creeper; the dark green of the one, and the many-coloured festoons of the other, were lovely indeed in the autumn.

But there were two other doors in the room. That on the left hand side as you stood facing the windows was always locked; it led into a spare room, which, like some eighteen or twenty others, was never occupied. This room had no exit upon the landing; it formed the corner of the north and east sides, and probably was used formerly as a dressing-room of Alice's room. Now, however, the room which was entered from her bedroom through the door on the right was used by her as a dressing-room, being much more convenient for the house-maid. You could pass through it either on to the landing, or straight into the apartment occupied by one whom everybody called "nurse"—a worthy family servant of the good old-fashioned type. Alice once said to me, "What is it which makes one take nurse's unimpeachable trustworthiness for granted? It isn't her face exactly; I think it must be her cap!" I laughed at the dear girl's odd idea, and agreed that it *was* her cap, and also her mittens and her shawl. "One would trust her with unlimited plate-chests," said Alice. "And unlimited babies and young footmen and housemaids," said I; "not that babies seem to have been her special attribute, though I believe she was nurse to Mrs. Crighton Lewis' two little children at one time. They died when they were tinies, as I daresay you know. I rather fancy the title 'nurse' comes more in connection with her talents in the sick-room sphere."

"Very likely it does, for I know she presides over a medicine chest big enough for the requirements of a man-of-war's crew![2] She asked me to help her dust and wipe the bottles one wet day in the spring, and I was astonished at all she told me about the drugs. She seemed as clever as a chemist! I wondered then if the late 'Mr. Nurse' was a chemist and druggist, but I did not like to ask her."

"No, dear, the late 'Mr. Nurse,' as you call him, was named Simpson, and he was a gardener."

"Nurse is very kind to me. She scolds me a little sometimes, to be sure, if I get my feet wet, or forget to wrap myself up enough, or if I sit up late at night in my bedroom; but her scolding is meant very kindly, and shows she really tries to look after me for my good.

[2] Man-of-war: a powerful, armed warship or frigate.

I have a strong liking for nurse. I am quite sure she is fond of me."

But I am digressing most unwarrantably, and must take up the thread of my tale again.

The previous night, after the customary gathering of the household at nine o'clock for prayers, Alice had gone to her own room with the delightful sense of having performed all her little duties well, and the intention of enjoying a short time to herself, gleaned from her sleeping hours! Putting on her dressing-gown, she sat down to finish some work, the first piece of really elegant needle-work she had ever done; none but the very plainest had ever been given to her to do during her life at Ailsbury. It was simple but tasteful, an embroidered frock which she hoped to send off the next day to Mr. Griffith's eldest daughter, whose home was now brightened by a six-weeks' old son!

The time slipped away; Alice worked with all an industrious, neat-fingered girl's enjoyment of a "nice piece of work." The last stitch was set, the frock was held up for final scrutiny in case some tiny detail should have been omitted, when she heard a slight noise at the door on the left hand side of the room.

Looking up, she saw it was partly open, and a *hand* was on the framework high above the lock, as if someone was steadily pushing the door against some resistance, and was about to enter. She started up in great terror, staring fixedly at the *hand* all the while, and moving sidewise, without taking her eyes from the *hand*, towards the entrance of the dressing-room, and called or tried to call, for the word seemed to die in her throat, "Nurse!" Then, while she was gazing, the hand vanished! "No, it was not taken away, it disappeared, it slowly vanished, *slowly faded away!*"

She was quite sure she had not looked away from it for a single instant!

CHAPTER II

HER terror was great. She dared not alarm the house, but in an agonised voice called, "Nurse, nurse!"

At last the old servant came, sleepy, stupid. They looked at the door. Was it open? "No," nurse said (rather crossly); "it's all your fancy, Miss Alice; why do you sit up till near twelve? If you was a-bed and asleep, as you ought to be, you'd never hear nothing of the kind."

They tried the door; it was firmly closed as usual. Alice, half-ashamed, begged nurse to stay a little while. Nurse dragged a table before the door, and herself finished undressing Alice and put her to bed. She then fetched a spirit lamp from her own room, and warmed up the cup of chocolate which was standing on the little table by the bed; Alice, when she went to her room, in her haste to get on with her work had forgotten to drink it. Nurse then opened the shutters, so that the clear moonlight might be a comfort to her young friend. Alice soon fell asleep, and slept calmly the rest of the night. There was no sign of the past fright in the morning, except that she felt rather less bright and alert than usual.

Well! truly here was matter for reflection. Being a calm, unexcitable person, I told Alice that my opinion was that it was a case of burglar, *not* bogie! The very telling her story had relieved her, and I soon saw that her belief in the supernatural nature of the sight she had undoubtedly witnessed was wavering. It appeared to me that the most prudent thing for us to do was to consult Mr. Jones, a highly respectable policeman whom I knew very well. We agreed to do this, and to abide by his advice as to the advisability of alarming Mrs. Crighton Lewis or not. I knew Policeman Jones' ways pretty well, having almost *lived* at his house during his poor wife's rheumatic fever last winter, and felt tolerably sure we should find him at home that morning.

I quickly put on my bonnet; though no longer young, I am not given to loitering when I have made up my mind, and we walked down to the village. Mr. Jones was at home, and Alice at my request told her tale.

I perceived that his interest was at once awakened; there were no signs of an inclination to sneer, no lazy suggestions of "a dream, maybe." He plied Alice with questions as to the position of her apartment, what other rooms were in the immediate neighbourhood, what she knew of their uses. Then, opening a locked drawer, he took out one or two papers, and after looking at them for a moment or two he made a few pencil notes on the margin of one of them—which proceeding rather excited my impatience, it seemed so irrelevant, and almost as if he were only giving us a divided attention. He said:

"If we can manage this business quietly without frightening Mrs. Crighton Lewis, we will. She is getting on in years now, and a fright or trouble would be very bad for her, might give her a stroke like. And there's other reasons besides. Don't you say nothing to nobody, miss. You won't, will you?"

Alice readily promised, but shyly expressed a hope "that she would not have to sleep in that room alone again to-night."

"If you do, miss, you shall be well looked after," he said. "Did you ever happen to see Mrs. Crighton Lewis' beautiful old plate?" he asked.

She replied that "nurse" had spoke to her of it, and had told her she would show it all to her some day.

"Did Mrs. Crighton Lewis speak to you about it?"

"Yes—I think she did. She was present, I know, when nurse promised to show it to me, for I remember her saying I ought to ask nurse to show me how to clean it, for she knew how to do it beautifully, and it was a useful thing to know, as I should find when I had a house of my own; it was Mrs. Crighton Lewis saying that which makes me recollect her being there."

Jones and I knew that the Crighton plate and jewels were of great value, and were supposed to be kept at the manor house.

Jones then said that he would contrive to call on me at about half-past two o'clock, when he would have finished what he had to do that morning, and he hoped by that time he should be able to arrange something to make miss a bit easier like in her mind.

"Can she be there too, miss?" he asked, "I should like to talk to her about what I wish to do."

Alice said she would ask leave to come back to me punctually at that hour for the avowed object of learning how to knit a quilt, which Mrs. Crighton Lewis wished to work, and which I had undertaken to teach her some days ago.

As we walked towards home, Alice said after we had been some time silent, "Aunt Lucy, I think the policeman is on your side of the question in 'Burglar *versus* Bogie,' and I am glad, though I cannot quite shake off the peculiar terror of seeing that hand vanish."

We then parted; Alice, light of limb, running up the path through the ferns, under the dark green pines towards the old manor house; and I, soberly, taking that which soon brought me to my cottage home, and to my arm-chair again in the library.

Scarcely was I seated when a rapid knock, followed by an energetic pull at the door-bell, disturbed the silence of my abode!

"Such an unnecessary expenditure of sound with the implied

intention of gaining admittance to my modest dwelling," thought I, "when he, she, or they, have only to turn the handle of the door and apostrophise the handmaiden, who certainly would be in sight through the half glass door of the little room at the end of the tiny hall which serves as pantry and still-room in my establishment! It must be a stranger!"

Not a bit of it! An active step sounded in the entrance, and in walked handsome Frank Wagram. Well, that *was a contretemps!* Frank *is* my nephew, my only nephew real or supposed, though, as I said before, I have plenty of make-believe nieces. In a corner of my old heart there is, I fear, a worldly little fold! I am conscious of the hope that Frank, now a rising young barrister, will find a well-dowered bride, and I do not wish him to meet my pretty little Alice until, if it may be so, he is betrothed to a certain young lady who just meets my views!

However, what with my pleasure in the sight of his honest face, what with listening to the expression of his joy at finding his old auntie at home, and of his undoubting delight in the satisfaction it must be to me to receive his unexpected visit, I had no time for prudent thoughts and considerations, and it was almost one o'clock before I began (while Frank was writing a "business letter," which was the supposed pretext of his journey down to Crighton, about something I had consulted him about, but which the dear fellow could just as well have written in his chambers in London, only he had persuaded himself that his auntie wanted stirring up a bit), before I say, I began to wonder if I could not put off Alice and Jones, and defer the "Burglar *versus* Bogie" case till to-morrow, when all unannounced, in came Alice, looking her brightest, not seeing Frank, who was sitting at the table. She ran towards me saying, breathlessly:

"Oh! Aunt Lucy, Mrs. Crighton Lewis is quite pleased for me to come; she is so kind, told me I might come back to you at once, says her poor head aches, and she is glad to stay in bed, for she was really only going to get up because she thought I should be lonely if she did not come down to luncheon. So here I am, all ready for the quilt and—"

The flow of words was brought to a sudden stop by the sight of Master Frank, who had risen and noiselessly approached my chair. There was now no help for it, so I introduced the young people to each other.

Frank had delightful manners with everyone, and certainly not the least with fair young ladies. He expressed great satisfaction at his own good fortune in choosing a day to come and see me when I had a visitor, etc.; told Alice he had often heard of Aunt Lucy's latest acquisition in the way of a niece, wanted to know if *he* was a cousin! in which quality he insisted she should immediately help him to unpack the little hamper of hot-house peaches and grapes he had brought down from Covent Garden, "to teach auntie to be a little greedy," he said.

His fun and chatty talk went on all the pleasant luncheon-time, and if Alice still looked grave now and then, her silvery laugh sounded merrily enough, and certainly she would not have given anyone the idea of a girl who had seen a ghost in the night!

When the appetites gave signs of being appeased for the present (and the ducks and green peas were things of the past, and the ham looked somewhat ashamed of itself), I said, "I don't want to hurry you, my dear Frank, but I must tell you something serious, and if you will kindly listen while you finish that cream, it well be as well, for I am expecting someone almost immediately on the business I am going to tell you about, and we shall want your opinion."

He made a little grimace, and said something about "things serious being very bad adjuncts to whipped cream. Did I wish him to add salt or mixed pickles to it, so as to be in keeping with my tone?"

But he knew how to be serious, too, and he listened in silence to my story of the ghost. After my first few sentences, he listened is stillness also. He did not laugh; but after hearing me to the end, said quietly, "This must be thoroughly looked into. I am doubly glad I came to-day."

Punctually at half-past two o'clock, Jones arrived. I think I had never realised before what a comfort it is to have a man belonging to one to help one. And such a man! Even if we had been less personally interested in the question, it would have been a pleasure to listen to my clear-headed Frank talking to the intelligent policeman. They seemed to understand each other at once.

By and by Frank said, "I see, Mr. Jones, that you have definite grounds for suspicion of certain persons. Probably you have a plan. Let us hear what it is."

"Well, sir, so I have; but, with your leave, ma'am and miss," turning to us, "I don't think I ought to explain it all, and name names as yet. Perhaps miss here (if you approve ma'am) will promise to carry out the little plan I have made without wanting to understand more about what I mean to do than I feel I can explain to her now? Do I speak clear enough, miss?"

Alice looked at me, and then said, "I will do exactly what you think right, auntie, whether I understand the reason or not."

"Then, my dear, you shall do what Frank and Mr. Jones will tell you."

"They may count upon me, auntie."

First, Jones cautioned her against any change in her usual habits, particularly in her manner towards nurse.

If nurse asks her, she is to say, laughing, "That she does not feel quite so silly to-night, and shall not sit up working in her room again."

Jones insisted on the necessity of averting suspicion in the house, for he, like many other "guardians of the public peace," chronically misdoubts those "extra respectable old parties," which expression of his feelings roused Alice to an indignant defence of nurse, and a recapitulation of her many virtues, winding up with a declaration that though she would do exactly as he had told her with regard to nurse, "that he would see!!" I fancied that I saw Jones exchange a look (of the nature of a wink) with Frank, quite unobserved by Alice.

Finally it is arranged that Alice is to go home in time for dinner, and act just as normal. She is to retire at the accustomed hour, and as soon as she is in her room, she is to slip the bolt of the dressing-room, to prevent nurse coming in, which she occasionally does (this she had told Jones, in answer to one of his questions in the morning). Then she is to draw up the blinds of both windows, in order that her light may be visible from the outside. That is to serve as a signal. Immediately Policeman Jones is to rear a ladder to the window nearest the dressing-room. Alice is to softly open the window (which she will have unfastened before dinner to avoid the noise it might make), and to step out on to the broad coping-stone, which, as I said before, runs along the whole side of the house directly under the windows, and then to descend the ladder. They are not afraid of nurse hearing, for she has been getting a little deaf for some time past, and no one sleeps on that side of the house.

Alice *said* nothing, but looked a little blank, so I put in a word. "Is the ladder quite safe, do you think?"

Reassured instantly by both the men, "Not the least danger. One of us, if needs be, will ascend and help her, while the other holds the ladder steady at the base."

Alice reminded me that she knew very well how to get up and down a ladder, when her "study" was in a loft. "It was not that she feared."

"Of course, Alice," I quickly added, "*I* shall be there, too, in the garden, and you will come home here with me at once. We shall explain all to Mrs. Crighton Lewis, *if* necessary, and when necessary. I know her well enough to be quite sure that she will be very grateful to us for having tried to spare her anxiety and worry, even if it should turn out that our trouble is all for nothing." (I said this last speech to console Alice, who was, I perceived, still sore at the implied suspicion of nurse's discretion, though she forbore to speak again about it.)

That was all, so far as her part and mine were concerned. When she would be safe off under my escort the police would keep guard, and from the position of the windows and the situation of the pine trees opposite, etc., we knew that it would be easy for watchers to see all that went on. As Jones admitted that he had other "lights" besides those we had thrown on a subject which had engaged his attention for some time past, and considerably more than suspicion as to a certain "party," we were fain to rest content, and suppose that all was for the best.

CHAPTER III

JONES took his leave, and Frank went out with him, saying he must "toddle" down and send a telegram to the effect that he should not return to London for perhaps a day or two.

To see him strolling leisurely along the road, his hands in his pockets, and a cigarette in his lips, no one would, I think, have supposed that the minds of the two oddly-assorted companions were strung up to a determined course of action, in which very serious consequences were involved, and which, perhaps, might not be without personal danger.

Not being as young as I used to be, I was rather weary with the unwonted excitement, and I daresay I *did* fall asleep over my knitting, as many other old ladies have done before me.

At any rate, when I roused myself, and had pulled my cap straight, and picked up the knitting-needle which I perceived shining on the carpet at my feet, Frank had returned, and was eagerly talking to Alice. The two seemed to be closing some arrangement, for I caught the words in Frank's voice, "Don't forget the cap; don't be in a hurry; Bob has a weakness for pretty caps, and, above all, have unlimited confidence in Bob!"

"Bob," said I, half awake, but speaking emphatically, "*the man's name is Jones;* you know how much I dislike slang."

"Oh, Aunt Lucy!" cried Frank, in his merriest voice, "surely you do not think I mean the bobby? I did not know you were so well up in slang!"

"Well, yes I did. Who, then, is 'Bob'?"

Thereupon Frank related the plan which he had induced the

policeman to allow him to graft upon the one already voted. Alice was to gain possession of a large pasteboard figure-head, which nurse used when making up her own highly respectable head-gear; she was to array this figure-head in a charming night-cap (Frank was extremely particular about that, declaring that "Bob" was endowed with discriminating taste), and place it in the bed, carefully arranging the pillows.

Then Alice was to step down the ladder to meet me, and her rôle would be over; as soon as she was gone, Frank was to mount the ladder, carrying "Bob." "Bob" is a bull-dog of unusual strength and intelligence, whose obstinate adherence to his own view of *duty* was above all praise. Once convince Bob's intelligence, and you may trust him to the death! Bob was at that particular moment engaged crunching bones, which he had graciously accepted from Alice's hand on the occasion of her being presented to him in an outhouse at the side of my cottage, in which retirement he had been placed on his arrival with his master, who well knew my objection to dogs in general about the house, and to bull-dogs in particular!

The introduction to Bob had been effected during my little nap. Frank would only need to show Bob the figure supposed to be asleep in the bed, explain to Bob that it was his duty to guard it, and then descend into the garden and join the police.

To avoid needless repetition, I will only say that Alice obeyed the instructions she had received to the letter; she reached the ground without accident. We entered my house as the clock struck half-past ten. Next morning we learned the subsequent events of that never-to-be-forgotten night.

Restless Frank soon got tired of "mooning," as he called it, in the garden (Cynthia, the changing luminary of the night, was not yet risen, and the sky was cloudy).[3] He determined to clamber up again; he slipped along the coping-stone, passing the windows of what we will now call "Bob's room." Sagacious Bob had but one idea—he was to guard that figure, so he did not trouble his head about the rustling ivy and the sound of footsteps, or, more probably still, he was well aware it was only his master.

Passing Bob's windows (Frank had ascended from just under the window of the long closed room which formed the north corner, on account of the strong ivy plant which grew under it) he reached that of the dressing-room out of which nurse's room opened. The window was only lightly fastened; he noiselessly pushed back the bolt with the blade of his knife, and gently raised the sash. ("I have often thought what a good hand I should be at a burglary," said Frank. "Now I *know* I have missed my walk in life.") I fancied I heard Alice demurely ask if there was not a proverb about setting a thief, etc. Pretty well that for timid little Alice! but these supplementary remarks were added a good many months later, not on the morrow of the tragedy.

He stepped into the room, and as he did so, a low, very low, growl caught his ear, then a rustling sort of dash, and a horrid snap, then a stifled groan of agony . . . . Frank tried to open the door leading into Bob's room; forgetting the bolt Alice had been told to slip, of course it resisted his efforts. With instant energy he got out of the window again, ran along the coping-stone, imitating the whistling cry of a night-bird, which was the concerted signal to the police below, and climbed into the room. There he saw in the dim light of a cloud-streaked moonshine a *man*, and Bob with a mortal grip on that man's throat!

[3] Cynthia: another name of Selene, Greek goddess of the moon.

Quicker than words can tell, Jones was up the ladder, followed by two more policemen. In a moment handcuffs were on the man's wrists, then the faithful Bob released his hold, and after shaking himself, settled down again by the pillow to guard his "trust," keeping, however, the corner of one goggle eye on his half-choked victim, and grimly wagging his stump of a tail in polite apology to his master for not having completely strangled the intruder while he was about it!

Evidently the burglar had expected to find Alice asleep in the room when he noiselessly entered. The sudden and effectual attack of the dog, and the pain when his fangs entered and tore the flesh, had made him incapable of getting at the revolver he had in his coat, or of drawing out the knife which he carried like an American at the side of his trousers' pocket. Had he done so, alas! for Bob!

"Well, all is up now, I s'pose," said the burglar, as soon as he recovered his breath; "but, Mr. Jones, don't you be too hard on a poor fellow till you hear all about it; and look ye, if ye want to get what's left of the 'stuff,' you'd better look sharp after old Mother Simpson there! Look in her room, and in the box under her bed, and the basket in the cupboard, if you want a paying job. It's all her doing. I'm glad I'm caught, and it's all up—I was only to get enough to pay me out to 'Merica—she'd got all the real swag—b'lieve me or not as you like—please yourself—but it's gorspel for a' that!" He relapsed into silence.

Just at that moment a noise at the dressing-room door caused one of the policemen to unfasten the bolt, and open it, admitting—nurse! She entered excitedly, saying "Where's the young lady? Miss Alice, dear, where are you? I won't have you frightened, my dear." The words were hardly uttered when once more Bob sprang from the bed, and flew at the old woman. He seized her dress, and glared at her, with the evident intention of making a dash at her throat if she stirred. Frank called off his dog, and Jones, taking nurse by the right hand, forced her to sit down upon a chair. Bob planted himself in front of her, his gleaming blood-red eyes fixed full upon her. Meanwhile one of the policemen had procured a light. Jones still held nurse firmly by the wrist. She tried to wrench her hand away from him, crying, "Where is Miss Alice?" Then catching sight of Frank, "Who are you? Where do you come from? Speak to me, has anything happened to Miss Alice?"

Frank answered her, pitying rather the poor old thing, with her grey hair hanging in disorder down her shoulders, "No, no, Miss Alice is all right; she went away a long time ago; she knows nothing of all this."

The burglar cried, "Hold her fast, Mr. Jones; she's got the swag! the old hypocrite!"

The woman still struggled to release herself. Jones said, "Come, old lady, it's my place to make sure of you; p'raps you can clear yourself, you know; don't you go for to say nothing as will be used against you!"

She sat quietly for an instant, casting a look of intense detestation at the wretched man, who was trying to wipe his bleeding throat with his handcuffed hands, and who returned her glance with compound interest, while he railed expressions of the direst hatred at her. Frank, in spite of his first movement of pity for her, began to think she did indeed look a most villainous old person; the expression of her distorted features was positively murderous as she cursed the burglar in her rage, and not only the burglar, but his mother and his father, and their masters and mistresses! Suddenly she broke off, and turning again to Frank, she asked:

"Did Miss Alice suspect me? Did she plan this against *me*, I ask you?" Assured that Alice had never entertained a moment's suspicion of her, "Though *we* know what we are about, old lady," put in Jones, she went on to say rapidly, "Then I was right, she was real good—yes! yes!" To the burglar (whom one of the men called Jim), "I know the game's up, and if you were to swing for it I would not care, only not for *her*. . . . Yes, yes! (to Frank)—"I'm all he says, and more"—she laughed here; "but I couldn't have borne harm to happen to that young girl. I heard the noise, and I was a-feared for her; you would not, maybe, have found me out if I hadn't come in. Well, well, well—let my hand go, policeman. I'll not struggle again, I'm tired; I'm old now; I feel main bad, main bad; let my hand be; I want to get out my salts as is in my pocket."

In truth she spoke thickly, and was white and livid as a corpse. Motioning to one of the men to pass him a glass of water for her, Jones relaxed his hold, still keeping his hand ready to seize her arm again if there should appear to be any need to do so.

Nurse drew a wide-necked smelling bottle from her pocket, and after fumbling, like a person who is sick and faint, with the stopper for an instant or two, opened it, but instead of simply smelling at the contents of the bottle, she put it to her lips and rapidly poured them down her throat. Then, muttering something which sounded like, "I don't believe in nothing against her!" dashed the bottle at Bob and fell back—dead!

CHAPTER IV

BOB'S usual calm did not forsake him; the bottle fell over him, a few drops of the liquid it contained wetted his coat. He did not even turn! he only sniffed and sneezed and then yawned emphatically!

Jones and Frank consulted together as to what was now to be done. They decided to call up the servants. Jim, the burglar, who was well up in the geography of the house, indicated to them where the footman slept. The man was soon awakened, and by his help the women were roused. The scene may be more readily imagined than described. When nurse's body had been laid upon her bed, Frank advised that the cook should undertake the task of going to Mrs. Crighton Lewis' room, and of telling her as gently as possible that a misfortune had happened to nurse, with the intention of getting Alice to tell her the rest of the events of the night later on. Cook remarked that it was very strange that Kate, the servant who slept in Mrs. Crighton Lewis' dressing-room (since nurse had begun to grow deaf) had not heard them all getting up at that unwontedly early hour, two of the other women servants sleeping close by on the same floor; "and she such a light sleeper usually." Kate did not appear to be a light sleeper to-night. She lay, when the cook came in, in such a deep sleep, breathing so heavily, that the cook said to herself, "Surely she must be drunk." Drunk the poor girl was not, but she was drugged. Cook remembered that nurse had said to her, just before bed-time, that Kate had a cold, and that she should give her some of the same posset which her mistress was in the habit of taking at night, as "it would never do for Kate to be coughing and sneezing, and waking missus." The cup stood near the bed, and when it was examined later on, the few drops which remained in it were proved to contain a powerful narcotic.

But the worse was to come!

Mrs. Crighton Lewis lay motionless on her pillow! No need to tell her what had occurred! She would never hear aught again in this world! The victim and the poisoner, the generous benefactress and the recipient of her almost life-long bounty and kindness slept their last sleep under the same roof!

Nurse had also drugged her posset, but with the same direful potion contained in the bottle from which she had just drunk herself! Truly that was an awful night!

Alice's sorrow and emotion at the news of the death of her kind friend may easily be pictured. Nurse, too, came in for a share in her grief. She *could* not believe that nurse was such a monster as Frank's recital would prove her to be!

As may readily be supposed, we all had a great deal of trouble in piecing together and understanding the series of events I have just recounted.

It all seemed such a jumble! Had nurse gone suddenly *mad* with crime? *Why* had she done this? Where was her connection with the burglar? Who was he? What had he to do with her? Why had she drugged Kate and poisoned her kind, trusting mistress? We were all in a most terrible state of uncertainty. Jones himself could throw very little light on the subjects which puzzled us so. He had, "from information received," suspected Jim for some time past of being "up to something" beyond pilfering, for which he had a certain acknowledged reputation, though Mrs. Crighton Lewis would never allow any one to punish him if she could help it, being disposed to look on him as half-witted, and also because she had a very kind recollection of his dead mother. But he could not make out, if, indeed, Jim was after "big game," what he did with the proceeds, and that put him on the scent of nurse.

"Always turn the *unlikely* people over in your mind," said he. I really can only compare our mental state, for a few days, to what I suppose must have been the feelings of the Egyptians during the plague of darkness. Dread, fear, consciousness of some terrible evil, uncertainty, and horrible, horrible confusion!

Light, however, was at last thrown on the fearful tragedy, partly by what came out at the inquest, partly by the revelations of the burglar himself, who seemed positively thankful to have been arrested, and of others who had played a part in the past history of Crighton Manor and its inhabitants.

I will give the explanation as briefly as I can before closing my little tale.

Many years before the date at which my story began, James Simpson was head gardener at Crighton Manor. He was a remarkably handsome young fellow, extremely intelligent, in fact, possessed of unusual ability. He was steady and hard-working. He was very young to have so responsible a place as that of head gardener in such an establishment as the manor house then was. He owed it partly to his own merit, and partly to the favour of the lady of the manor, who had her own views concerning him.

Mr. Crighton Lewis was alive at that time, and the nursery was gay with the sound of children's voices.

The upper nurse, Anne Fuller, was rather young also for her position. She was a clever, bright girl, and coming often into contact with James Simpson when playing in the grounds with the two little children, it came to pass that she fell in love with the good-looking young man.

He had a very pleasant, hearty way with him, and always seemed pleased to see her; she persuaded herself all too easily, it appeared, of what she wished to believe, and *felt sure* that she was only returning his affection when she suffered her heart to go out to him.

There was an under housemaid in the family named Mary Clark, a girl of about eighteen. Mrs. Crighton Lewis regarded her with especial kindness, for she was the orphan girl of the nurse who had taken charge of her when her own mother died, and her grateful, loving heart felt pleasure in showing kindness to Mary Clark for her mother's sake. She was well worthy of her kindness, for she was good, and faithful, and true.

Mrs. Crighton Lewis formed the project of marrying Mary Clark to James Simpson, having discovered that she was by no means indifferent to the young gardener's attractions.

One morning she sent for him, and mentioned the subject to him, entirely ignoring that it was an open question whether he was becoming attached to Anne Fuller or not. Perhaps it was a case with him of "How happy I could be with either!" Perhaps he really did prefer Mary, and only waited for a pretext to make up his mind between the two, or possibly the intention which Mrs. Crighton Lewis somewhat prematurely announced to him of giving Mary a marriage portion of £100 influenced him. Certain it was that he fell in with the proposal, and then and there, in his mistress' presence, asked Mary Clark to be his wife.

A few hours later, Simpson met Anne Fuller in the grounds and accosted her with the words, "Well, Miss Fuller, has Mary asked you to come to our wedding next month?"

The shock almost gave Anne a fit, but her pride kept her up, and choking back her emotion, she managed to reply: "No, Mr.

Simpson, but I was expecting she soon would, and I'll be delighted to come, and will get a new gown on purpose."

Deadly hatred to little Mary took possession of her heart. At the wedding, though as pale as if she had had a severe illness, Anne was outwardly brave; but instead of prayers she muttered curses on the blameless young bride. None the less bitter did Anne feel when she knew the extent of Mr. and Mrs. Crighton Lewis' generosity to the young couple. The marriage gift of £100, the pretty furniture, the dress and linen, and the increase of Simpson's already very good wages. The Crighton Lewis family knew no sweeter pleasure than that of brightening other people's lives.

Within a few short years, pretty Mary Simpson was buried under a green hillock in the churchyard, leaving a baby of a week old, and an elder boy of three years old. Simpson was broken-hearted at first, but after a while seemed to find comfort in talking to Anne Fuller. His old feeling for her revived, and he asked her to marry him.

"I know," said he, "you'll love poor Mary's baby, and the elder one, too, for I believe you loved little Mary."

Anne secretly wreaked her spite on the baby (James). Nevertheless he contrived to live and grow up. Two or three years after their marriage Simpson died. Mrs. Crighton Lewis, now herself a childless widow, allowed Anne to continue to live at the lodge of the manor house with the younger child, she having expressed her wish to bring him up. She had a special satisfaction in using poor Mary's belongings.

John, the elder boy, a clever, good lad, went to his grandmother, old Mrs. Simpson, who lived down in the village, and who sent him to the school.

Jim grew up clever in *some* things, but the neighbours were wont to declare, "not quite sharp either." Frightened by his step-mother, who, though she contrived never to be unkind to him before witnesses, was almost insane in her manifestations of aversion to him when alone with him, Jim was *not* like other boys. The one good influence on his head and heart was his boundless love for his brother. As soon as he was with him the cowed, anxious look which made some people regard him almost as an idiot, entirely disappeared. John used to say to the clergyman sometimes, when he spoke of Jim's dulness, "Oh, sir! if you could see him when he is alone with me, and isn't frightened!"

One day, when Jim was about fourteen, he came into the lodge and cautiously laid on the table, drawing them one by one from his pocket, four eggs.

"They be quite fresh," said he.

"Where did you get them from?" said Anne Simpson, less sharply than usual.

Very slowly Jim replied, "I *found* them, mother."

They had a nice dish of poached eggs for dinner, and Jim had his full share of the little extra. After the meal Mrs. Simpson took his arm firmly but not unkindly, "Look at me, James; if ever the police or anybody *catches* you a-robbing hen roosts or aught else you'll have no mercy from me. Do you understand?"

"Yes, mother, I knows. I shan't get caught; anyways, if I does, you don't know nothing 'bout me nor my ways. I'm a bad 'un, I am!"

From that day Jim received better treatment, and many a nice fowl, or fat duck, or hare appeared on Anne Simpson's table. She rejoiced at seeing Mary Clark's son grow up a thief! She delighted to see him pilfer and rob the mistress who had portioned Mary Clark! Little by little she had grown to find pleasure in scraping and hoarding up. Many a time the poor lad half resolved to own all to John, and to forsake his bad ways, but the dread of his step-mother held him back, and she had a way of pushing him to evil, the influence of which he felt but could not explain, much less resist.

Time went on, and John emigrated to America. From time to time he wrote to the clergyman, sending kind messages to his brother. Jim could not have read his letter himself, poor, neglected boy! On the death of the housekeeper, Anne Simpson left the lodge, and came up to live at the manor as housekeeper and "nurse" to Mrs Crighton Lewis. Jim was taken on as odd boy about the stables. He rarely did any work, but just idled about the fields and woods, and preferred eating scraps and broken meat anywhere about the place to taking regular meals with the servants. He grew more and more silent and shy; but nurse never lost sight of him, and he continued to be her tool in carrying out sundry thefts, which she plotted and contrived, while all the while sustaining her character for fidelity and trustworthiness. She never forgot her rancour against Mary Clark, and against the mistress who had been so generous to her. She never forgave Mrs. Crighton Lewis for having promoted the girl's marriage, and patiently waited for revenge. Years only increased her thirst for vengeance and gain. Insanity alone can account for it. Over and over again she repeated to herself the proverb, "With time and patience the mulberry leaf becomes satin," until her whole life became bent into one wicked groove.

Mrs. Crighton Lewis, as she advanced in years and became feebler in health, trusted more and more to nurse's care. She had the keys of everything, and the charge of all the valuables. By degrees she abstracted all the silver from the large chest, except a few of the larger pieces.

Jim used to creep into the house, and secrete himself in the room which I have described as forming the north-east corner of the house, which communicated by means of a hidden staircase and a disused door with a place which had served long ago for a bath-room on the ground floor, and which had an egress on the garden, by which, before bath-rooms were constructed in their present perfection, water was probably carried in to supply the bath. The windows of this room were closed by thick shutters, which were kept bolted, as the place was supposed to have been unused for years. He used to pass through Alice's dressing-room to gain access to his step-mother's apartment (as I think I said before), and fetch the silver and other objects of value, and convey them to an individual who used to meet him at some distance; he then brought back the money received for them to his vile step-mother. With thriftiness and order worthy of higher things, nurse carefully laid up the money; some was in the bank, some well invested, and a good deal hoarded up in her boxes. She had promised Alice to show her the plate in Mrs. Crighton Lewis' hearing, expressly to avert suspicion from herself in case of the disappearance of the contents of the chest being accidentally discovered.

The night of the catastrophe was to have been the last expedition of the kind. The last fine old silver heirlooms would have found their way to the smelting pot. Nurse had put a sleeping draught into the cup of chocolate which was waiting as usual for Alice, but which, naturally, she entirely forgot to drink in the excitement of preparing and effecting her Hegira![4] Many times already she had had recourse to this plan for enabling Jim to pass

[4] Hegira: a journey, especially one taken to escape from a dangerous or undesirable situation.

and return without disturbing the young girl's slumbers. Had Alice drunk her chocolate on the previous night *before* beginning her work, instead of letting it get cold, she would never have seen that ghostly hand!

The question will be asked why Mrs. Crighton Lewis had not been poisoned on that first night? It is impossible to decide that with certainty. We know that great sin presents itself to the mind by degrees. Perhaps the unhappy woman only conceived the idea of putting the climax to her revenge at the very time she accomplished it. Perhaps her mind had become finally unhinged from its own weight of evil. In any case Jim most certainly had no idea that poisons were any part of the scheme.

Nurse had gladly closed with the stipulation he had made, that she should give him money and clothes enough to enable him to go to America out of the proceeds of this last haul. But more probably her plan was to have mourned with well-feigned sorrow the "death during sleep" of her mistress in the morning. She would have accounted for the absence of the plate, when it came to be discovered (which it might not have been for some time, as the heir-at-law to the property was in a remote part of India, as she well knew), by declaring that Mrs. Crighton Lewis had taken it herself to London by instalments. She did take very heavy luggage with her, the contents of which nurse (who always accompanied her) alone was acquainted with.

It would then be supposed that she had deposited it with a banker. Time would be lost in trying to discover which banker had received it, and Jim would be off before suspicion was awakened; and when he was safely out of the way, she would be free to enjoy her dishonest gains, without fear of discovery.

If these were the misguided woman's calculations we have

seen how they came to nought, thanks to Jones' cleverness and promptitude of action.

Touched by the frankness with which poor James Simpson, now relieved from his life-long terror of his step-mother, confessed to his share in the misdoings, and taking into consideration the cruel treatment by which the fiendish woman had incited and forced him to evil for her own vengeful ends, my nephew undertook to defend him himself at the assizes.

Strong in his conviction of the sincerity of Jim's resolve to reform his life, Frank dwelt so earnestly on the above considerations in his address to the jury (as well as on the practical point that it was through Jim's voluntary avowals that a great part of the property was recovered) that his pathetic appeal for mercy was responded to by the twelve good men and true who were listening to him. Jim was sentenced to six weeks' imprisonment without hard labour. The prison chaplain's instructions completed the good begun; better feelings and aspirations began to take root in the heart of poor Mary Clark's son, and at the expiration of his punishment, Frank saw him on board a Transatlantic steamer, on his way to join his brother and begin his new life.

I may here say, that all those who interested themselves in the poor fellow were well rewarded by his excellent conduct, and by the useful life he led when once more under the influence of his dearly loved brother.

One more word before we finally take leave of our reformed burglar. When privately questioned by Alice, on the eve of his departure, about the "vanishing hand," he replied, smiling:

"Oh, miss, I were a-watching of you through a crack in t'door; I see your eyes fixed on my hand, so I just scratted the hinges of the door; your eyes wavered like, just for a moment, *though you didn't know it yourself*, and my hand was gone![5] 'Tis a trick I learnt," he added, "a-watching of the birds and creatures in the woods, and all about."

Kind Mrs. Crighton Lewis had, it seemed, entertained a presentiment of her approaching end; for, nearly seven months before, she had added a codicil to her will, by which she left to me, in trust for Alice Taylor, the sum of £5,000, and all the money which might happen to be to her credit in her banker's account at the time of her death. It so happened that several large sums had been paid in a few days before the sad event, and thus Alice turned out to be the heiress of over £11,000.

Mrs. Crighton Lewis' original plan had been (with the aid of Mr. Griffith, who, you will remember, was the clergyman at Ailsbury, where Alice used to live with her uncle and aunt) to go thoroughly into the details of the deaths of Alice's parents, and find out if she was indeed so completely "a beggar" as her aunt delighted to tell her. They were privately conducting the inquiry by means of Mrs. Crighton Lewis' lawyer. Evidently the good lady feared she might die, and leave Alice again to the tender mercies of her aunt, before the affair was brought to a satisfactory conclusion. She knew, indeed, that I should take the dear girl to live with me; but she feared, on the one hand, that she would be a burden on my not very ample means, and, on the other, she knew my reasons for not wishing to renew my acquaintance with Mr. Griffith, estimable and worthy man though he was.

I may as well give those reasons here, and thus explain my emotion when the dear child first asked me if I had ever seen *a ghost.*

[5] Scratted: scratched or scraped at with fingernails.

CHAPTER V

THIRTY years ago—yes, as long ago as that, ah me!—the prim old maiden lady known as Miss Lucy Wagram to her little world in general, and as "Aunt Lucy" to her young friends, was a bright, happy girl, on whose sky no cloud had passed! I was engaged to be married to Theodore Griffith, the curate of a distant parish, and deeply did I respect him, and truly, truly did I love him.

We had a large Christmas gathering at home. My dear father's house was filled with guests. Theodore, of course, was staying with us. We were to be wedded in the first week in January.

A thoughtless girl (I have forgiven her long ago. *She* never knew—oh, no!—she never knew what suffering came of it! a thoughtless girl, I say) fancied it would be fine fun to dress herself up as a ghost, and, with the aid of one of her schoolboy brothers, to give Parson Griffith a fright! She succeeded in mystifying him, and he thought it right to say a few words to my father on the subject.

My father, as I learnt afterwards, was fully persuaded that Theodore had had a dream, but he forbore to tell him so. The accomplices in that foolish joke were on the watch. They observed Mr. Griffith's grave face as he left the study, and caught sight of the quiet smile on my father's face as he turned away.

That night she played the same trick! This time Theodore was not deceived; he saw it was a girl—and—fancied he recognised *myself!*

Angry at having been made a fool of, as he believed, by me, indignant at what he thought my unmaidenly conduct, he immediately packed his valise and left the house, and thus never learnt that the silly girl had also terrified me, literally almost to death!

The effects of that terror, and the pain when I read the upbraiding words of the letter Theodore left for me, his expressed determination never to see me again . . . . brought on congestion of the brain, and my life was in danger. I recovered my reason, but a not very unusual effect of the illness remained—I was afflicted with a most pronounced and hopeless squint. I am used to it now, but I felt it bitterly then.[6]

I was wrong, perhaps—I think not, however—but I never could bring myself to consent that any attempt should be made to bring Theodore and myself together again, though I knew he had been set right as to the identity of the "ghost." I preferred he should think I was irreconcilably offended—what he would, in fact.

I *could* not have borne to see him avert his eyes, those eyes whose loving glance I had so often shyly met, and which I so loved secretly to recall to myself, and how could he have helped it? Ah me! ah me! Well, well, we shall none of us squint in heaven!

Now, however, now we are old, we shall probably meet again. It turns out that Alice's aunt *has* money, and a very nice sum of it, too, which she holds in trust under her husband's will for Alice—money which she will be obliged to make over to her when the dear girl will be twenty-one, or when she marries!

"Of course she will marry Frank!" Don't be in such a hurry; she will do nothing of the sort. Theodore Griffith, *junior*, a clever but somewhat impecunious young solicitor, has long pitied and secretly cared for the lonely little girl. He dreamed about her when he was at school. Long ago he confided to his sister his cherished hope of one day "rising" in his profession, and asking Alice to be his wife.

---

[6] Squint: also called strabismus, where the eyes are not properly aligned and point in different directions.

Alice suspected the existence of these sentiments, but had never alluded to him to me. She "dared not think about him," she said; "there never seemed a ray of hope;" and even at the time she was speaking there was no dawning ray, but *now*, with part of Alice's money, and by the practical help and advice of Frank, who said he felt more than ever a cousin, a capital partnership is to be procured for young Theodore in an old-established firm; and the day is not very distant when Frank will be "best man" on the occasion of Alice's wedding.

N.B.—I am gradually accustoming myself to wear large, green, cage-like spectacles, with hinged flaps at the sides. I shall dispense with them after the wedding. I am foolish, perhaps; never mind! After all, I am only a woman!

A CLEVER TRICK

AND

WHAT CAME OF IT

A CLEVER TRICK
AND
WHAT CAME OF IT

CHAPTER I

ROBERT Graham had just landed from the P. & O. steamer at Southampton. He was in early middle age, broken in health, lonely, and a disappointed man.

At a comparatively early age he had won a distinguished position in the Indian Civil Service, and in due time married a very beautiful girl, to whom he was deeply attached. Laura Greville had a "good fortune," as the phrase goes, and notwithstanding the drawbacks entailed by an Indian life, their marriage was extremely happy, only shadowed by the deaths, one after another, of four children.

At length another little girl once more brightened their home, and she seemed so much more robust than the others had been, whose brief lives had only been counted by weeks, that the parents' hopes revived, and the little Ella became their darling treasure and mutual joy.

For the first five years of her young life not a shadow crossed the happy daily path; but ere long the clouds began to gather, and the baneful effects of the Indian climate were seen and felt, for Mrs. Graham's own health was also failing; so, very reluctantly, she returned to England, taking with her the precious child.

Robert Graham, with firm and stoical self-denial, would not then apply for leave of absence from his post.

He knew that such absence would postpone the completion of the term of service which must take place before the retiring pension could be granted. If he left India for a temporary absence now there would be delay, since the time spent on furlough would not count in the Civil Service, and he was fervently anxious for the day when he might retire, and enjoy what would be his first real *home*, where he should be free from the daily routine and anxiety of his profession, and safe from the risks of a tropical climate and the other trials which so seriously affect an exile's happiness.

But from the time that Mrs. Graham left India, nothing but sorrow and wearying anxieties crowded into his life.

True, the letters which reached him every week from England told him ere long that their little Ella was daily growing stronger, daily more winning; but though Mrs. Graham made light of her own increasing weakness, she could not conceal the fact that the state of her health was unsatisfactory. And yet, when at length she owned the truth, worded as tenderly and considerately as possible, that the deliberate result of the medical consultation was the verdict, "May, *perhaps*, linger more than a few weeks," the shock to her husband was terrible; and when the next mail brought the sad tidings of her death, Robert Graham broke down utterly. He felt stunned at first; then it seemed to him as though he had heard the news weeks ago, and had been in a delirious dream ever since.

Time went on, but he never recovered from the blow; and his own health gave way under the pressure of the sorrow which he must bear *alone*. Ere many seasons had passed, Robert Graham was obliged, to his own bitter disappointment, to send in the resignation of his post fully five years before his length of service would entitle him to the hoped-for retiring pension.

"To save your life," were the words of two experienced doctors.

So Robert Graham took his passage to England, leaving India and his once bright hopes for ever.

When, after a night passed at the Southampton Hotel, he entered the railway carriage on his way towards "home" (he always said that word with a tinge of bitterness in the tone), he had intended to travel in a carriage with no other occupants, and esteemed himself fortunate when the door was closed on him alone, very shortly before the fixed time for starting. His destination was into a rural district near Gloucester. The house, by name, "Woodleigh," was, however, only known to him by report. Mrs. Graham had settled there when she returned to England. It was her own property, inherited from an uncle some time after her marriage. She had often described it in her letters, with loving hopes that her husband might soon come there, telling him of many arrangements she was making to enhance his comfort, and dwelling on the joy with which all should be prepared to greet him.

Alas! all was now over.

How he blamed his own short-sighted folly. Why had he not, like other men, taken a leave of absence, and thus enjoyed a respite from toil? why had he gone on, obstinately believing in his own powers of endurance, trusting to his own bravery, buried in the daily routine of work, putting aside the needful relaxation he sorely required, and so in his blind folly losing all he aimed at?

Vain regrets now, and he knew it. His little Ella, too, she would not know him, she must be almost seventeen now. Was she thinking lovingly of him? Was she watching for his return with happy expectation? The thought gave some comfort.

Just as the train was on the point of starting, an officious porter suddenly opened the door, saying, "Room here, ma'am," and in jumped a girl of about 18 years of age, followed by a lady in deep mourning. There was the customary hurry and bustle as the incomers took their places, and the porter evidently felt some disappointment when a trivial twopence came instead of the silver sixpence he had expected. The twopence was given with a sweet smile and a profusion of thanks. Evidently he had rendered unusual services on the lady's behalf.

Mr. Graham buried himself in the morning papers.

By and by some slight incidental act of courtesy passed between the ladies and himself, and he soon found himself in full conversation with the mother.

She was exactly what one would describe as a comely woman, with a singularly attractive and winning manner. Her sparkling black eyes and clear brunette complexion struck him as very pleasant. It never occurred to him that the sparkle of those eyes *might* flash out in anger!

How could he suppose that intimate friends had even whispered that the gentle-mannered lady could be, as one of them had said, a very "tiger-cat" at home!

She was so gentle, yet so bright, and gradually Robert was drawn deeper into conversation, and learned with real pleasure that the lady lived not many miles from Woodleigh, and then heard, by a most singular coincidence, her name was *also* Graham!

The little lady was, in fact, the widow of an extremely distant relation—indeed the distance was so great that only the proverbial clannish instinct of a Scotchman could have detected the kinship between Mr. Archibald Graham, deceased, and the retired Indian judge now on his way to Woodleigh.

"No!" she had never seen Woodleigh. She had only lived at the *Dene* one short year—and that was a year of deep anxiety; her "Dear Archibald" had died above eighteen months ago, and she then could not stay *there* where everything reminded her of her loss. She had been "so crushed, so ready to die with the burden of her loneliness all the first year, and could not now have roused herself but for the thought of her child—that had drawn her back to life once more . . . . " More such remarks followed, and Robert found himself sympathising in kind words, and then *she* was so tenderly murmuring words of sadness. *She* could so well understand the hopeless loneliness! and the bright eyes shone through unshed tears. It was not long before the end of the journey was reached, but ere they left the train Mr. Robert Graham had energetically and with deep earnestness planned that Mrs. Archibald should come over two days hence to take luncheon at Woodleigh; "our girls," he said, "will soon be fast friends."

When Graham reached his house, he met a sweet, shy, but very loving welcome.

Ella had grown tall, though slight and elegant, and oh! so like her mother!

Was it a strange fickleness, or was it not rather that under-current of sadness *too real, too deep for words*, that *pain* of sorrow which seems as if it must *hush itself* lest the aching heart should break?

Aye! what was it that made Robert Graham experience a *sort* of annoyance that Ella should so forcibly remind him of her mother?

Explain it as you will, the fact was so. He shook off the feeling, however, and roused himself to draw his daughter closer to his heart, and he managed to talk during the dinner with tolerably well-feigned interest.

So the evening passed away, and the wearied traveller withdrew to his room, and soon sank to sleep.

His sleep was troubled—dreams haunted him with an undefined sense of change. Old scenes of his early boyhood mingled with immediate circumstances. And once he awoke, and found he was uttering the words, "What a charming person!" (probably the fascinating little Mrs. Archibald Graham was the "charming person" of whom he was dreaming?)

The acquaintance between the families of Woodleigh and of the Dene rapidly ripened into friendship. Why be slow to tell what my reader has guessed.

In six months from the time that Robert Graham had landed at Southampton, a lonely, broken-hearted man, Mrs. Archibald Graham had become Mrs. Robert Graham, and the retired Indian judge was no longer *lonely or broken-hearted*—at least, if *once broken*, it was now whole! And Ella and Mabel called each other "sister."

Robert Graham lived but a few years after his return to England, always more or less an invalid during the time. His wife tended him with every care, and, as increasing weakness drew on, her really skilful watchfulness was most helpful, and when all was over she wore the very deepest crape costume, and mourned as a "twice bereaved" widow in the most graceful toilet that fashion would permit.

Whether her heart mourned, who is to decide?

Ella was about twenty-one years of age when her father died.

To say that his marriage had really increased her happiness would be too strong an expression, but Mrs. Graham was kind and cheery, and, perhaps, Ella's natural timidity helped her, for she was very willing that the task of arranging everything to please her rather capricious father should be taken from her, on whom the burden had weighed painfully, and undertaken by the brisk little lady who had, as her friends said, "quite a gift for managing a household."

In due time the kind old family lawyer had a private interview with Ella, when he explained to her very carefully her position. She had now by right of inheritance the entire control of all her own mother's fortune. It was considerable, amounting to little less than £900 per annum, besides the house and land at Woodleigh, which the solicitor estimated should, if she let it, bring in not less than another annual £300.

Then he explained in clear, concise words than in justice Mrs. Graham must either pay Ella rent for Woodleigh, or seek another home.

But Ella had learned that the widow had inherited *nothing* from her first husband, for "poor Archibald," as she always styled him, had died without a will. Consequently, as he left no son to inherit his estates, all the landed property from which he had derived his income passed to the heir-at-law, who, being a needy man, took his "rights" without a thought of the widow of his distantly-related cousin.

CHAPTER II

MRS. Graham now, at the death of her second husband, was left with a small income from the marriage settlement which her first husband had made, and a life-interest only, to the value of about £150 per annum, under Mr. Robert Graham's will; he having no property, could leave his widow only what he had saved. Ella, therefore, positively refused to ask or to receive rent, but told Mrs. Graham that she sincerely hoped their home might not be broken up, and that as long as the widow was content to remain at Woodleigh she must feel as if it were her own in every respect, Ella undertaking only the payment of all expenses. "I do not forget," she continued, "all your kind, unselfish care of my dear father through his long and painful illness," accompanying her words with a cordial grasp of the hand.

The years they had all passed at Woodleigh had been very pleasant. Country friendships are often more hearty than those in the more numerous circle of town acquaintance generally appear to be. And among many true friends whom Mr. Graham had found when he settled in his English home, none had become more intimate in the family than John Brownlow and his sister Ruth. The brother and sister shared a picturesque farm residence about two miles from Woodleigh, and Robert Graham found much solace during the weary hours of his long illness in the frank kindness and cheerful society of John Brownlow, and very few days passed without some interchange of visits between the families, for Ruth very quickly made her way into the inner circle of the affections of Ella and Mabel, and soon shared in all their excursions, picnics, and other amusements of country life.

John was an excellent specimen of an honest-hearted Englishman, "true to the core," as the saying is; but his excellent qualities of intellect and heart were all sadly marred by a constitutional shyness and reserve, which seemed at any important crisis always to come to the front—and that to his disadvantage!

Ruth, older by some years, was almost like a mother to her idolised brother; she had resided with him and managed his household ever since their parents' death.

When at length poor Mr. Robert Graham died, the sorrow at Woodleigh naturally drew the two families closer. The sympathy of the brother and sister at Newbould Grange cemented the firm friendship, and Mrs. Graham also shared in the happy intimacy. And so it came naturally to pass that the first topic in the discussion of the day's plans was generally connected with the Brownlows.

About a year after Mr. Graham's death, the two girls were returning from a long walk, and quite unexpectedly met their friends, the brother and sister from the Grange. It was a most lovely evening in early summer, and the friends joined company to prolong the enjoyment of the fresh and fragrant air. Naturally, in the narrow country lane all could not be close together, and they fell apart; Ruth with Mabel walking on in advance, Mabel in eager discussion of some debated scheme, John and Ella following.

How it happened Ella could never clearly recall to mind, but some words fell on her ear from her companion's lips which set her heart beating! The words could not be mistaken as to their meaning, shy, nervous, but distinct—but before she could frame her reply, Mabel had suddenly flown back to them in half real, half feigned terror, at a wasp which she declared was attacking her.

The interruption was complete. Only a quiet pressure of the hand, and they parted.

But *those words!* Ella repeated them silently in her heart of hearts. She was strangely disturbed with the new sensation. Could it be, she thought, could it really be that all the cold weight of loneliness was removed. Her young heart had been so long oppressed with the blank, the utter desolation, which had reigned there since her mother's death. She was full of deep, silent joy, mingled with tender earnest prayer for him whose name she yet hardly trusted herself to breathe.

The next day was more than ever lovely in its summer brightness. The girls spent all the morning in the garden, and Mabel seemed surprised and somewhat annoyed to find Ella in such spirits. She was so much brighter and happier than she had been since her father's death, and cheerily flitted hither and thither, carrying out the light horticultural duties in which she delighted—all pleasant, all self-imposed, and in which Mabel generally shared; but to-day she chose to sit quietly with her book under a tree whose spreading foliage afforded a deep shade.

After a longer interval than had previously occurred, Ella passed by where Mabel was sitting, and as she went along, was singing, or rather carolling, in a sweet, clear voice, to a lively tune in which tender notes intermingled in the somewhat irregular strains.

The words seemed to be part of an impromptu song.

"Why, Ella!" interrupted Mabel, rather pettishly, "where did you learn that nonsense?"

"Ah," said Ella, "I think it is very happy nonsense, without a thought to sadden it. I overheard our little Maggie singing over her dairy work some words of nonsense very like it—and, perhaps, I caught the infection."

This was the song, to which we may give the title:—

SONG OF A HAPPY HEART

"Oh! my heart is gay
As the flowers in May,
For I heard him say—
Yes! I heard him say, 'I love!'

"Ye linnets and blackbirds! sweet twittering throng,
Now cease for a moment your chorus of song!
Say, pretty birds, say!
Did *ye* hear him say 'I love!'

"Then all the birds in the happy throng
Gave answer in tuneful cheery song—
Oh! his voice was soft,
And his voice was low,
And the tone of his words was earnest and slow;

"But borne to us on the fragrant breeze,
Rustled the words 'mong the leafy trees—
For the voice of love
Ever mounts above!
And *we* heard him say, on that summer day,
'I love! I love! I love!'

"Then happen what may
My heart must be gay—
For they heard him say—
Ah! *I* heard him say, 'I love!' "

But noticing that Mabel was decidedly cross, Ella quickly slipped out of her own merry mood, and soon contrived, dextrously and gradually, to smooth the ruffled temper. Ere long, all was bright, and they began to arrange for a long-desired excursion.

Ruth, they knew, was unusually busy just then, so they would go alone. They would be "out" all day, would take luncheon with them, and go by an early train to X——g Heath, then through the copse to Fl—— Castle, and ramble to their hearts' content amid the ruins.

When they announced their plans to Mrs. Graham, they told her they did not intend to return in time for dinner, but that supper about eight o'clock would be very acceptable.

The next day was perfect in beauty, and they started as they had arranged, for the delightful trip.

To tell the truth, Mrs. Graham found their day-away-from-home very opportune. She sent a kind message to them by her maid in the morning, saying that she had not slept well, should therefore take breakfast in bed, and hoped they would thoroughly enjoy their ramble.

She told the maid that she should not dress that morning, but would remain upstairs and merely have a slight luncheon in the dressing-room, and keep very quiet.

She had a tiresome headache, she said; and really in her elegant robe of soft pearly-grey cashmere she looked quite an invalid!

The real state of affairs, however, was this—Mrs. Graham sorely needed a quiet day, free from possible interruptions. She was harassed and perplexed.

Before her second marriage she had by degrees involved herself in money difficulties. From time to time she had borrowed various sums, amounting at length to a very considerable amount, for owing to her "dear Archibald" having died intestate, she had been left with a mere pittance for the support of herself and her child—the small sum which her own father had given her, and which Archibald had settled on her. Her father had died soon after, and died poor.

Mrs. Graham was one of those people who never have an idea of self-denial or true economy. She had contrived to pass a good deal of time with relations; "living on the enemy" she called the plans by which she secured food and a roof from the somewhat unwilling hospitality of all on whom she could quarter herself and Mabel. Hence, when her friends' patience was exhausted, and she was obliged to return to the Dene, her speedily-following marriage was a most fortunate relief to her finances, and while Robert lived she had contrived to pay the interest on the loans with tolerable regularity. She had never dared to own her embarrassment to him, because she had told him (with a winning falseness which was habitual to her) that, though "sadly poor, she was never in debt!"

At the present time there were heavy arrears, and her shrewd lawyer, having ascertained how straightened her means were likely to be in future, had addressed a polite but emphatic letter to her on the subject, and this letter had reached her on the previous day. She *must* reply; she must *think* how to do so.

Therefore when her simple luncheon was over, she bade her maid give the message that was to be repeated to any persons who might call that day—"That Mrs. Graham was lying down with a severe headache, and that the young ladies were gone out." "No matter *who* may call," she added with emphasis.

Lying on her couch with the professed intention of sleeping, but with her mind far too anxiously preoccupied for that to be possible, she was revolving what scheme she could concoct which might help in this emergency, when about three o'clock she heard the sound of wheels, and glancing out from beneath a safe concealment she perceived John Brownlow in his dog-cart, overheard his voice, but not the words. She noted that he seemed to linger more reluctantly than necessary for a mere inquiry, then at length drove off.

Mrs. Graham rang her bell sharply. The maid entered with letters and the message that Mr. Brownlow had called, and seemed disappointed, left the letters, saying he should very soon call again, repeated his regret at hearing of Mrs. Graham's indisposition, and had driven off without saying more.

The maid asked whether, as there were three notes, she should take the two which were addressed to the young ladies, and put them into the library, to await their return home.

"No; leave all three here for the present, and bring up the tea-tray. I shall take a little tea, and then go to sleep. Don't let me be disturbed after you have brought up the things on any account whatever."

The tea, etc., was duly brought in, and the maid retired.

With much more alacrity than her languid tone and manner would have led one to expect, Mrs. Graham rose from the sofa and sharply looked at the door. Then taking the three letters she closely inspected them. One, addressed to herself, she opened first; it was a card of invitation to a garden party for next week from Mr. and Miss Brownlow. The other notes were for Ella and Mabel. What evil spirit made Mrs. Graham examine these so closely?

Mabel's was evidently just like her own, the card of invitation; but that for Ella was very decidedly a *letter*, not merely the pretty card of the others.

A sore temptation came to open that letter—simple curiosity at first, for she was always inquisitive especially about trifles.

She put it aside, however; no doubt Miss Brownlow had written about some of the many topics of mutual interest; she often did write to the girls.

Then the widow took up both letters again, and it suddenly occurred to her that it was a very singular and unexpected fact, that the addresses on both the girls' letters were in Mr. Brownlow's hand-writing and only the letter addressed to herself was written by Miss Brownlow.

Why should *John* write more to Ella than to Mabel?

What *did* it mean? She flushed suddenly as she thought—can John be seeking to win Ella?

Here that mischief-loving sprite made her picture a different case! "What if John should marry Mabel!" she murmured to herself, "He is so rich!" Oh! if it might be, all her money troubles could be postponed—might, by and by, be cleared away.

The seed thus sown sprang up rapidly. She hardly expressed to herself the full import of the idea that presented itself—but said, aloud—"Of course I can open my *own* daughter's letters." . . .

How handy was that hot water, on the tea-tray! . . . almost without difficulty the adhesive envelope was unclosed. She had been right. Mabel's letter only contained the card of invitation. The temptation to open *Ella's* letter now became quite overpowering. That envelope also yielded to the skilful manipulation. There was the card of invitation to the garden party, and *a letter* . . . .

It proved, as Mrs. Graham had expected, a fervent expression of love; but the hope that such a boon, such a priceless boon as that he asked, was expressed in a half-desponding tone—yet, *might* he hope?

It was awkwardly worded, almost abrupt at the close—"Now, dearest Ella, answer me—may I hope? etc., etc., etc."

Mrs. Graham rose in strong agitation from the table, and impatiently paced to and fro. She took that hated letter from her lawyer from her desk, and read it over again. With studied politeness he wrote:—"I am most reluctant to press this matter on your immediate attention, but I must frankly own that unless you can furnish me with some reliable security, my client will shortly insist on repayment of the loan, with the accrued interest." Then followed the figures of amount she must repay, etc., and some polite, but meaningless expressions of sympathy and wish to be of service.

. . . . . If Mabel were to marry John Brownlow, would not *that* give the required security at once! a wealthy son-in-law, undoubtedly? If Ella was his choice, could her stepmother count on help?

No, she could see no hope. Then, too, Mabel had always been a trouble, a great expense, and she was really so anxious about her future.

Here the evil spirit whispered, "Can't you change the envelopes?" How fast her heart beat! She could *hear* its hard, rapid pulsations! For a moment she tried to suppress the thought, but then began to parley with the unseen foe.

"I don't believe Ella would ever care for plain John Brownlow," she murmured; "he is so blunt and awkward. And then what a blessing for Mabel! she so sorely needs a firm, kind guardian. Already she is beyond my control, and is *such* an expense—quite a burden on my poor income. Then, too, if Ella refused him—and I'm sure she *would*—what a trial to that dear, shy, worthy fellow!"

Again she took up the cards; each had the name "Miss Graham" only, added in manuscript to the usual lithographed form of invitation, but the envelopes were carefully addressed—

Miss Ella Graham.

Miss Mabel Graham.

The lady placed a card again in each envelope, then took *the letter*, and read it carefully.

"Dear Miss Graham,"—nothing could be more fortunate, but the closing words caught her eye, and her hopes faltered.

These words were, as we have seen—

"Now, dearest Ella, etc." . . .

Once having *willingly* lent her ear to the aforementioned sprite, she could not prevent the whisper—inaudible but *very real*, that followed.

"You are very neat, very dexterous; how easily 'Ella' would alter into 'May.' Why, there is the very word just below! You *are* skilful; you could just scratch out the top of that 'E,' and add the 'y' at the end." The temptation was very sudden; it was plausibly followed by another whisper—"After all, it is for the good of all. Mabel will make a charming bride; she is far handsomer than Ella. It is *really* for their good." So evil prevailed. That cunning interpolation of "a good motive" cloaked the wickedness of the treachery.

I could well-nigh believe that the evil sprite had held that sharp pen-knife! so lightly, so effectually the *E* disappeared, and now only *Ma* was left. Mrs. Graham quickly added the *y*, and the whole word, *May*, stood out so clearly that John himself could scarcely have disowned the handwriting—why, the very space he had left after the word (which he *had* written), in his nervous agitation, was all in favour of Mrs. Graham's purpose!

CHAPTER III

IT was done. After an evil deed well and successfully accomplished, there may follow, *for a time*, a bold sense of satisfaction.

With a brilliant flush on her cheek, Mrs. Graham closed the two envelopes. "Courage, courage, I have done it very cleverly, and then I know it is for the good of them all."

THEN SHE SLEPT.

How easily we may slumber under the cold shadow of sin . . . . but will there not come hereafter an awakening?

Towards seven o'clock she rang her bell, and desired the maid to help her to go to bed. She was better, but only fit for quiet rest. Then she added, "Take the note that is for Miss Ella, and let her have it as soon as she comes in, and tell Miss Mabel to come to me as soon as she has had supper, for I have a note for her also."

The girls reached home very soon after, and during supper Ella told Mabel of the garden-party invitation, and they knew the second card would be found in Mrs. Graham's room.

They parted for the night. Ella went up to her room, though it was a little over eight o'clock—but she knew Mabel would remain with her mother, and it was very lonely downstairs.

Bright the thoughts that filled her heart. Presently the very natural idea came—just a feminine perplexity—on the subject of *dress* for the garden party. "What shall I wear?" Then she recollected a certain white embroidered dress, which had never yet been made up. It was of an exquisite Indian material; her father brought it home, and some time after his return had given it to her. (Ella never knew that he had previously presented it to Mrs. Archibald

Graham when they were affianced! but the lady had refused it, it did not suit her style, she said, and suggested that he should give it to his daughter.) Yes, she would have the Indian material prepared for the coming occasion.

Next she opened a letter which had arrived during her absence that day. It was from Miss Randall, the true friend who had cared for her, and superintended her education during her mother's slowly-failing life, and had remained with her at Woodleigh up to the date of her father's return home.

Miss Randall had a keen insight for Ella's somewhat difficult position, now that her father was dead, and now wrote to tell her, that a length of long-desired pleasure was possible—a foreign tour. For recently she had inherited a moderate competency which would allow the indulgence, and she had arranged for a long and delightful tour, and added, "I think, dear Ella, you may not be unwilling to leave home for a while, and I am sure it will be beneficial to you. Will you join me? But I must ask for a quick decision. Let me hear from you within three days."

How delightful this plan would have been a short time ago!

Now—well! she would wait one day, a letter written *then* would be in ample time; and if "those words" were as much in earnest as she believed . . . . of course she did not wish to hurry away from home.

So Ella quietly rested, happy and at peace, and slept soundly.

Let us now go back a little in our story and follow Mabel, who, when she bade her sister good-night, went to her mother's room.

Mrs. Graham, with strong self-control, was calm, and took interest in the history of the day's little picnic; then, in a careless tone, told Mabel there was a note from Newbould for her. Mabel rose and took it from a little side-table where it lay, saying, "Oh, it's a garden-party card—and mother! mother! you *must* let me have a new dress, I can't go in my *old, old* things!"

Mrs. Graham, while Mabel was still holding the unopened letter, replied that she *really* could not afford to buy any new clothes.

"You know I have very little money, and *you*—you are not like Ella, *you* haven't a penny, so don't worry me; I want to finish the paper I was reading before I go to bed." And taking up a periodical which had come that evening, she watched Mabel very closely from behind the shelter of the book.

The girl opened the letter, and drew out the card, read it, and looked pleased. About to put it back into the envelope; she gave a little exclamation of surprise as she found the *letter*.

Mrs. Graham saw her start; saw the sudden flush, the fixed gaze, the parted lip! "How pretty the girl is!" was her involuntary thought.

Mabel read the letter twice, then put it into her mother's hands without a word.

Very cleverly Mrs. Graham acted pleasure, but not surprise.

"Mother! I can't understand about it . . . . I never supposed . . . . I don't care a bit for him, in *that* way, I mean."

"Dear child," said the mother, in her most winning tone, "you are not the first girl to whom the open avowal of a long cherished love comes as a surprise, and yet," she added archly, "*others* are not surprised!"

To Mabel's hurried questions, Mrs. Graham said that *she* had guessed long ago; then one by one fenced off or softened the girl's objections—then, oh, how cunningly, led on to the thoughts of wealth, position, happiness: shed a few soft tears as she spoke of her dear, her only child, penniless! "and even at my death, you know there will only remain my own little all, for your step-father left me but a life-interest in the very moderate income he assigned for me. As John Brownlow's wife you could command comforts, money, admiration; you, my darling, will *then* never know the straits to which I am reduced." And so she flashed the ideas of dress, jewels, dinner parties, excursions, pleasures of all kinds, before the dazzled and bewildered girl.

Sure 'tis a sight to make the angels weep, when a MOTHER sows the baneful weeds of vanity and selfishness in her daughter's heart.

"What shall I do, mother?"

With crafty tenderness Mrs. Graham answered, "Let *me* send him a note—I shall only say, 'Come!'—and then all will be easy, all quite natural."

Mabel consented to this suggestion. Then after playing carelessly with the letter, she read it again. "Mother, it is so strange! I thought, I really *did*, that he was in love with Ella! do you think there can be *any sort* of mistake in our names? Really," she began again, "really, I've a good mind to ask him if he's sure he did not *mean* Ella!!"

"MABEL!" cried Mrs. Graham in a tone that made the girl quail; it reminded her of days, not so *very* long ago, when condign and sudden punishment had always followed that tone! "MABEL!" raising her voice to a yet sharper key, "if you *dare* to say such a thing to him, I will tell him about Signor Enrico."

Mabel was instantly cowed and silenced. This threat alarmed the poor girl. There had been in her *early youth*, while she was at school, a very silly unladylike act, really nothing more grave than a piece of naughty daring, originating from older companions, joined in, and actually carried out by Mabel from sheer love of mischief, without the least idea that any trouble could arise from the trick they had planned.

As far as Mabel was concerned, the result was only a very severe punishment from her angry mother, who also removed her from school, and so cut short her education, which had been a real enjoyment to a girl of good ability for intellectual pursuits. But as she grew older, she had a morbid dread that the bit of childish folly might be viewed in a different light, and where she had at first only thought of it as a naughty freak, almost too severely punished, she now had an exaggerated dread of any allusion to the matter, believing—what was really a most ridiculous idea—that it was terribly compromising!

Therefore, when her mother so cruelly taunted her, the threat struck hard, and she sat sullen and disheartened.

Presently Mrs. Graham, dropping her sharp accents, gradually brought back the topic of the worldly attractions of the "match," and little by little drew the girl to a brighter train of thought, skilfully mingling tenderness and hope with a train of glittering fancies. Late on into the night they sat talking; then Mrs. Graham prepared some chocolate, and mother and daughter parted, seemingly trustful, loving, and happy.

Mabel's dreams, when at length she rested, were somewhat tangled and confused, but soon complete oblivion effaced all agitating memories.

She did not appear at breakfast. The servant told Ella that "Miss Mabel is taking breakfast with Mrs. Graham."

It was seldom that Ella had a long, quiet morning and it was very welcome that day, for she had an arrear of letters to look over, destroy, or answer—some to school-fellows who had married, some to school-fellows who had gone out to India to join their parents; and this quiet day afforded the required leisure to send off many of the most urgent replies. So the time passed away quickly. Sitting in the drawing-room, absorbed in her task, she once heard sounds as of some visitor, but took no heed.

Soon after midday, she went upstairs to her own room, having duly given out her letters for the post, and there, sitting by the open window, began for the first time that day to consider how she should reply to Miss Randall. She was very reluctant to disappoint her friend; but she did not wish to leave home *now*. She was weighing her words and framing a reply when, before her ideas had actually taken shape, Mabel briskly knocked at the door, and entered. Flushed, with brilliantly shining eyes, looking really beautiful, she came up to Ella, and in a strangely softened voice, said—"Say you're glad, Ella! say you *are* glad!"

"What about, May?"

Mabel, throwing herself into her sister's arms, replied—"John Brownlow has asked me to marry him, and I said, 'Yes!' "

Poor Ella! her brain reeled; it needed a strong effort to overcome the feeling of faintness caused by the sudden mental shock. Had Mabel been looking at her this would have been seen. But with a strength of will which surprised herself, so rarely had she called it forth, Ella recovered her own self-control almost instantly, and gently pressing the excited girl in her arms, she replied—"Oh, Mabel, of course, you know, dear, I love you like a real sister. Of course, your happiness must make me glad!" Silence and a loving kiss followed.

Then the volatile Mabel started up, seated herself by the window, and began to talk of the garden party. What dress could she wear? Would there be many people, and so on, until, to Ella's intense relief, she jumped up, and with a brisk "Good-bye," was off.

But let us go back and describe what had occurred since breakfast until Mabel rushed unto her sister's room with the unexpected news.

Quite early, Mrs. Graham had sent out a tiny note to Mr. Brownlow, and after breakfast descended to the library, which by tacit consent she now always used as her own private sitting-room. It was a pleasant room. A large bay window near the fire-place gave a cheerful view of the lawn and shrubbery, and was furnished as in a recess with a writing-table and its usual adjuncts. On the left-hand side of the room were folding-doors, which opened into a large conservatory; and when these doors were fully open the whole of the flower-laden bower was in view; but the doors were so contrived that when firmly closed no one in the conservatory could hear or see anything that took place in the library, and those in that room were equally secure, being unable to see or notice what was going on in the conservatory. Anyone might be safely ensconced in the further recess of the leafy shelter, and could also, if desired, at need, emerge unobserved by a side door into the garden.

When Mabel joined her mother in the library, the folding doors were only open in one half, and the soft breath of the flowering plants brought a soothing influence to both mother and daughter. They spoke from time to time, but not a word on the one absorbing interest. Presently the door bell rang. Mrs. Graham, kissing Mabel on her forehead, bade her go into the conservatory "until I call you," then firmly closed the doors.

She then quietly seated herself in a comfortable easy-chair (placed with the back to the large window), with a book in her hand—all so quickly that one might have thought she had not stirred from her place for hours!

John Brownlow entered. He looked pale and nervous; his old enemy, shyness, had evidently laid a firm hand on him.

Words fail me when I would describe the interview—the

widow's warm welcome, the tact with which she prevented the possibility of his uttering a word! or how, to his half-stammering efforts to explain, as he began to say—"But! . . . Mrs. Graham! . . . you must surely have observed"—she interrupted in the softest tones—"Of *course!* yes, of course! can you wonder? a MOTHER'S eye!—yes, a mother's eye saw it all." Then came a quick ripple of flowing words, incessantly murmuring kind things!

Oh, John! John! why? why did you not burst through that rapidly-flowing, gentle torrent—that artfully mingled and incessant stream of words? Why not abruptly stem the flood?

He was actually bewildered; she quoted words from his poor letter. A horrible nervous uncertainty hovered over him; he would have given anything to see the letter, but was far too embarrassed to ask for it. *We* know it would not have helped him! Then the thought—the strange thought—was it possible, that in his wretched awkwardness and agitation—was it *possible* that he *had* written the wrong name? or could he have put the letter into the wrong envelope? The rapid, ceaseless flow of Mrs. Graham's words—first gentle, then tender and loving, alternately cheerful and sad—so utterly confused him that he *could not* speak. And then she added—"This comfort to my heart for dear Mabel is all the greater, for I really thought once—but only for a moment—that you were attracted by my dear step-daughter." John started. "And oh! I am so glad you are spared a disappointment." Again poor John made an effort to speak. "Yes," continued the widow, "dear Ella's heart has been long and very worthily bestowed."

That dexterous LIE completed Mrs. Graham's victory. She had now quite secured her victim.

To such a shy man, to be refused for "another" would have been agony. As said Miles Standish, the redoubtable captain—

"I'm not afraid of bullets, nor shot from the mouth of a cannon,
But of a thundering 'No' point-blank from the mouth of a woman,
That I confess I'm afraid of—nor am I ashamed to confess it."[7]

Such were the thoughts of John Brownlow, could he have expressed his feelings so clearly.

He was stunned and dizzy, figuratively speaking, by the torrent of her (Mrs. Graham's) rapidly changing words.

Quickly, while he was still under the effect of the confusion caused by the blow so cunningly dealt on his sensitive heart, Mrs. Graham had opened the door that led into the conservatory, and said in sweet, cheering tones, "Mabel, my child, JOHN calls you;" then led the blushing girl up to him, placed her little cold hand in his, and with a loving word of congratulation left the room.

Could he, *could he*, COULD HE repulse the young confiding girl? That pretty, shy, blushing maiden? . . . . Truth to tell, he was startled to see how very charming she was, and a sudden feeling of mingled admiration and pity shot through his heart, so near akin to love that his embrace was very real, very cordial, scarcely shy.

Was Ella so soon forgotten? The lie which Mrs. Graham had forged, had it killed the scarcely acknowledged love? and thus the *new* love so quickly took its place!

I know not! hearts are fickle,—they need nourishment! Well! so it was.

---

[7] Myles Standish (c. 1584-1656) was an English military officer. These are lines from the poem 'The Courtship of Miles Standish' by Henry Wadsworth Longfellow.

CHAPTER IV

TO return to Ella. When her sister had shut the door and left her alone, the real hard wrestling with a rebellious, wounded spirit began. She laid her head down on her folded hands in bitter pain, mortification, and still harder self-rebuke.

Then the thought *would* thrust itself before her—"Oh, is Mabel worthy of him? does she care enough for him?" Then came the bitter conflict, lasting long. Wearied at length by the mental strain, she rose, and with faltering steps went to her wardrobe to take a handkerchief, and as she took it up she accidentally touched the white Indian material of the dress she had been thinking about so recently with such happy plans. With a suppressed cry of heart-agony she said aloud—"Oh, I cannot bear this! *This* must not go on; this is WRONG. The world was free for his choice—he had every right to prefer Mabel! Poor weak, foolish woman that I am! Why should I have been *so sure* that those words meant *me?* I must conquer this."

Then she went to the window. It was open, and she leaned forward, gazing on the distant scene; the softening influence helped her, and here came a few gentle, healing tears. From that window she could see some half-a-mile from the house the village church and quiet graveyard.

Years ago she had bidden the gardener to clear away several trees, that she might clearly see from this window the white stone which marked her mother's grave.

"Oh, mother, mother!" cried the poor aching heart, and as she breathed the plaintive words, the soothing tear-drops fell faster.

Gently sinking on her knees before the open window, she was quiet, almost motionless. But when at length she rose, she had conquered. The *full victory* was won, and a holy peace rested on her heart and spirit . . . . Very calmly, and with deep thankfulness that such a door of escape was open to her, she wrote to Miss Randall—"Most gladly I accept your plan. I cannot say more in a letter; but I ask a favour. I could not ask any one but you such an unexplained request. Will you write and beg me to come to you *immediately*, and make no allusion to this letter? Merely write as if it were a quite spontaneous idea on your part—just ask me to lose no time in joining you." She finished and closed the letter. Just as she had done so she heard Mabel's voice, and called her to come in. "May, darling, I want you to have this Indian dress made up for you. It is quite fresh and new, and I am sure you will like it for the garden party!"

"Oh, Ella! How very kind you are. It is so beautiful, so *exactly* what I shall like," said Mabel, with inexpressible delight . . . .

In due time Miss Randall wrote exactly as had been suggested to her, and when Ella announced the receipt of the letter, and said she should start the next day, Mrs. Graham could scarcely conceal her satisfaction. Ella's going away at once seemed to make it sure that no possible explanation could occur, since she could not see either Mr. or Miss Brownlow before she left Woodleigh.

As soon as Miss Randall's letter came, Ella wrote and fixed the next day to join her in London. Then a brief note to Ruth Brownlow, explaining why she could not be with them at the garden party, adding a kind message of congratulation on the subject of her brother's engagement to Mabel.

When the preparations for her long absence were arranged, and they were many, as to servants, bailiff, etc., she wrote a cheque for £200 to Mrs. Graham's order, and went down to the library, where she found the lady resting in her cosy easy-chair.

Was there a shade of embarrassment in her manner when her step-daughter entered? if so, it was not perceived. After a short pleasant conversation on the subject of the foreign tour, Ella at once spoke of Mabel's engagement, and before Mrs. Graham had time to reply, she went on to say, "I shall be absent from home, no doubt, when the wedding takes place, and I wish you to feel exactly as if this were your *own* house. I have left directions that any orders *you* may give for such little repairs or alterations in the arrangements of the rooms and furniture as may be necessary to make all perfect for the wedding party, breakfast, etc., are to be considered as if I myself had given such orders, and of course charged to my account, and I should like to be allowed the pleasure of giving dear May her trousseau, so pray accept my gift for that purpose," and she handed the cheque to Mrs. Graham.

It is needless to dwell on the great satisfaction with which the liberal gift was received, and even while her lips were uttering thanks and affectionate words, many thoughts were passing through her active brain, prominent among them was—how could she suppress from Mabel the *actual amount*, and so possibly secure £100 for that terrible lawyer! to whom she must absolutely write that morning.

Was it by instinct that Ella had divined that the *whole gift* would not be for Mabel? and, having that instinct, had decided to write £200, where her first impulse had been to make it more by at least another £50, if not £100. Perhaps so!

At any rate, after she left the library she sought Mabel, and a very happy half hour passed quickly, Ella, talking of her tour and probable long absence, and the many changes she should find on her return home, told also the substance of her conversation with Mrs. Graham, and as Mabel began to talk of her hope that her mother would be liberal in the trousseau gifts, her sister told her she had made a present of money for the wedding preparations, but did not tell the amount, but added in very sincere affection, "There will certainly be some little fancies which the prudent mother will say are quite unnecessary, so here is a little packet of bank notes. These are for you to spend in any such fancies—anything, in fact, that will add to your comfort, and relieve you from the fear of burdening your mother, for you know her income is but small; and, if you don't spend all, it will be nice to have a little pocket-money to start with—to buy postage stamps to write to me, for instance!" That was added laughingly, for she saw the girl was about to pour out thanks, and who does not prefer *love to thanks?* How the happy girl's eyes glistened with pleasure when, bye and bye, she unrolled twenty notes of the value of £5 each!

The rest of the evening passed happily and all too rapidly. Ella started by the earliest train, met Miss Randall in London as had been arranged, and after a brief sojourn to complete the final arrangements, the two ladies began the long-hoped-for tour.

The absence from England was prolonged for many more months than Ella and her friend at first wished or intended; partly from the enjoyment they experienced in the new and varied scenes—partly owing to a long and serious illness which kept Miss Randall a prisoner for many weeks in one of the picturesque places where they had stopped in the course of their wanderings, and then as Miss Randall was recovering, the doctor said further change was most important before returning home, so weeks became months, and still they lingered. The complete alteration of scene and thought had enabled Ella to obtain perfect mastery over her own feelings.

The pain of wounded affection was gone entirely, and she had enough good sense and self-control never to allow herself to dwell on the *bitterest part* of the trial, that most painful idea that it was her own vanity, her own foolish self-conceit, which had made her so ready to take to *herself* words, which she *now* felt persuaded, had only been meant to refer to her sister.

When at length, after two years, the travellers returned to England, Ella had no wish to go to Woodleigh, and therefore hired a small furnished house in the vicinity of the London parks, and pressed her kind friend Miss Randall to stay with her for an indefinite length of time, in fact until some decided plans could be made, for neither of the ladies had any special interests to induce them to choose any neighbourhood for their future homes.

While in London, Ella had the pleasure of a promised visit from Mabel. It was put off several times, but at last Mabel wrote to say she *really* needed a *long time* of London shopping! Would Ella receive her? After the first brightness of meeting between the sisters, came much to talk over—the more noteworthy incidents of the tour, and sundry adventures, all, however, very briefly alluded to in their conversations, for Mabel was one to whom the business of shopping represented a height of enjoyment hardly to be adequately described by calmer folks! Yet she seemed always wearied in the evenings, but generally appeared again in the morning full of energy for the "charming" pursuit of fashion, and in excellent spirits. By degrees, however, Ella was perplexed and pained by the fact which she could not conceal from herself that Mabel was greatly changed, and not for the better. The defects of natural character in her early youth were scarcely noticed, veiled, if not quite concealed, beneath her girlish frolicsomeness and very sweet temper. (Perhaps that easy temper was more carelessness and a degree of selfishness which made it "not worth while to quarrel!" rather than really good temper at the root.) She had always skimmed lightly over the surface of troubles, had easily won the love of those who only saw her in her best moments, and even those more close observers of her daily life found themselves making more allowance for her than for other people. "Every one likes pretty Mabel," was the verdict of society.

But now she was certainly much altered. There was increased pettishness, a strangely irritable impatience of the slightest opposition; the most trifling contradiction of her will would rouse her temper to a degree most disproportionate to the matter under discussion.

And, far worse, she had a disagreeable, off-hand way of speaking about her husband—it seemed as if she almost rejoiced at any opportunity of disparaging him, even to unfairness.

Thus when Ella suggested that the next time Mabel was desirous of coming to London, her husband should accompany her, and said she would be very pleased to welcome him, her brother, and to renew the old friendship, the reply was careless—"Oh! John is taken up with the farm, and those labourers. He is building new cottages for them, and more than half spoiling them and their wives. I always say I don't see why they can't be satisfied with what did well enough for their fathers and mothers. Oh, no! nothing would take John away from his charming oats and turnips!"

The visit passed very quickly. Mabel, volatile as usual, seemed to forget home troubles, if she had any. Her light-heartedness made her sister willingly believe that what had made her anxious was only thoughtless chatter, and a perverseness of disposition, which was not *now* for the first time exhibited! It might have been noticed many times in former days, had one ever cared to dwell on faults in the merry young girl.

And then, how could Ella, of the same age, and unmarried, usurp an authoritative style, and hint at a higher standard for home duties?

So Mabel went away again to Newbould Grange, taking no heed of Ella's gentle hints of anxiety for her happiness. She carelessly answered that she was happy enough, though it was horribly dull sometimes.

The next event was a most delightful visit from Miss Brownlow. With excellent good sense, Ruth, as soon as her brother's engagement took place, expressed her intention of staying at the Grange no longer than might be necessary to get all in order for the change. The house needed very few substantial repairs. The ugly old-fashioned papers, etc., must be replaced by the beautiful modern Renaissance of an *older* fashion. And so cheerfully did Ruth tell of her own plans for the future, that a casual observer might have deemed her indifferent to leaving the home of her life-time, and have thought she had no loving remembrance of the years during which her every idea had been to secure her brother's happiness to the utmost of her power . . . . How cleverly we all fancy we can judge our neighbour's feelings! . . .

For a long time Ruth had been anxious that John should marry, and when she suspected that Ella had become dear to him, she was delighted.

When to her extreme surprise she heard that he had chosen Mabel, a vague anxiety and disappointment oppressed her. It was not that she did not love and admire the young girl; in fact, as a companion in their excursions and walks, she admitted that Mabel was more amusing than Ella. Yet she had long cherished the hope that the latter would some day be her sister, while such a possibility regarding the light-hearted Mabel had never for a moment crossed her mind. But she soon overcame the disappointment, and rejoiced in sincere pleasure that "John will now have a real home."

The engagement was very short, and the wedding took place in less than three months after Ella had gone abroad. Miss Brownlow skilfully carried out all her brother's suggestions. The workmen did all with spirit and good will, for their master was universally popular, and he well merited the respect and affection with which he was regarded. When the newly-married folks returned from their bridal tour in Scotland, the old country house was really a beautiful home for the young bride.

Ruth had already finally quitted the Grange on a round of visits to friends, from whom, for various reasons, she had long been separated. Both she and her friends were very happy in this renewal of *auld lang syne*, thus freshly cementing former ties of relationship and love.

So she knew very little by personal observation of the home life of her brother. Whenever John and Mabel were incidentally mentioned she would simply reply to questions, seemingly unwilling to pursue the subject, passing off at once to other topics.

The visit to Ella seemed very brief, so fully was each day occupied. It was only on the last evening as they sat in the frolicking firelight (though the subject had long been uppermost in their thoughts), that Ruth began spontaneously to talk about her brother and Mabel.

By degrees, drawn on as it were by her own musings, for no questions came to interrupt her quiet words—it was apparent, more from a tone of deep-seated sadness in her voice than from any definite words—yes, it was quite evident that home life at Newbould was not happy.

The past two years had not brought joy, or peace, or contentment,

John had been always loving and most attentive, promoting Mabel's wishes in ever way, but she, almost directly they were settled at home, began to be wayward, pettish, and unreasonable; she was constantly wanting change and amusement, yet she had no real ground for her complaint of dulness. They had a large circle of friends and acquaintances; she had horses and carriages at her free disposal; there were dinner parties, luncheons, and other festivities from time to time.

But after a few months she began persistently to tease her husband to go abroad, not for a mere tour of a few weeks—that he was willing to do—but to *reside* in a foreign town. John, with a proper sense of a landowner's duties, who faithfully carried out his responsibilities to his tenants and labourers—John to be asked to "shut up Newbould Grange," and go and live in Paris and other foreign cities for *a year or two*. Nay! *that* he could not, he *would not* consent to do.

Then, too, Mabel would go off and stay with her mother at Woodleigh, often only telling her husband of her intention at breakfast-time of the day she started. All this came out by degrees. Ruth, as she said, knew all these details, partly from the tone of Mabel's letters—they were mostly hasty, complaining notes, which seemed dashed off as a vent to her temper—partly from reports which had reached her from time to tome, for, alas! the home disputes were no secret in the neighbourhood.

Ella listened with renewed anxiety, grieved to the heart that her dear "little Mabel" had so sadly changed.

When Miss Brownlow left, her destination was the Rectory in a parish almost twenty miles from Newbould. Mr. and Mrs. Reynolds were old and intimate friends of her brother and herself; they had known their parents also. She promised that she would write freely and confidentially, and added, "After all, I sometimes think we are unduly anxious; time goes on, and I trust and expect to find all has settled into a happier routine." And so for a time it seemed. The first letter was reassuring. The kind-hearted old rector fully believed it was but a passing phase of wilfulness—"Mabel had always been so much younger in character than in years. Time will strengthen her and bring out her really good qualities." Mrs. Reynolds added, "If only little footsteps were heard in the nursery! that would call Mabel out of *self*."

About six weeks after Ruth had left, Ella received a telegram one chilly autumn morning.

It was from Ruth—thus worded:—"Mrs. Brownlow has started with her maid for the Continent. Sleeps in town, and goes this evening to Harwich. Follow her. Stop her. Her husband is dead. She does not know. It was sudden. Will write you to Royal Hotel, Harwich."

Instantly, without allowing herself to yield to the shock of the tidings, Ella made all preparations, sending out to ascertain the starting hours of the various steamers. She then sent a message to a well-trusted young friend, who had, she knew, sufficient knowledge of business of all sorts to render him a very efficient helper in any case where prudence, good sense, and discretion might be required. Fortunately, Mr. Collingwood was free from pressing engagements, and very willingly accompanied her to Harwich. They arrived at their destination in excellent time before any of the Antwerp or Rotterdam boats were timed to depart.

Rooms were then engaged at the hotel to afford accommodation for all, since it was impossible for any of the party to leave Harwich, if not going on the steamers for the Continent, before the next day. Careful precautions were taken that no letter or telegram should fail of being immediately delivered.

They had some time to wait. The London train would not be in for more than an hour. It was a cheerless evening. Rain would probably soon fall, for the gathering mist was rolling into clouds around the setting sun, not tinged with beauty from his rays, but cold, dark, gloomy, suiting too well the uneasy anticipations which filled Ella's heart.

The steamers did not start till nearly midnight, but her anxiety did not allow her to wait quietly at her hotel.

Why is it, that although time will actually pass, and one event succeed another, just as quickly if we lounge quietly in our easy-chairs until the fixed hour strikes upon our clocks—yet we do *not* sit still in any anxious waiting time, but we feel we must hurry—arriving very much too soon at the spot where action is to be taken?

Are there any calm souls who *do* sit still in grave anxiety? Who *can* resist the impulse to start before the time? If so, do their hearts and pulses gallop as quickly as ours? . . . .

Wrapped in a warm ulster, Ella waited by the approaches from the station to the harbour. In those dimly-lighted broad spaces she had a dreamy feeling of pain. It seemed as if all *must* be a delusion. Could she be mistaken? What did it all mean? Her young friend, Mr. Collingwood, was watching nearer the wharf, lest by any confusion, or crowds, or the increasing fog, Ella should miss the traveller for whom she was watching. How dark, how dreary it was. Now and then she started forward, thinking she saw a familiar figure. At last, under the shelter of their umbrellas, in the now fast-falling rain, she descried two persons—one, she was convinced, was Mabel, the other, no doubt, her maid. It was an anxious moment, threading her way through the bustling crowd, the rolling luggage-trucks, and all the usual impediments to progress in such a scene. She hurried on, uncertain, but dreading to lose sight of them in the dim light. At last she caught up the two figures on the Rotterdam steamers' wharf, and saw that one really was Mabel! Dreading that even now some obstacle might yet cause them to elude her, she cried aloud in her agitation, "Mabel! Mabel! oh, STOP!"

The astonished lady turned round. Ella grasped her arm.

"Mabel, I have something very important to say! No! I can't tell you *here!* " in answer to Mabel's angry questions. "No! not *now;* you must come with me!"

With an impatient gesture, and shaking off Ella's hand, Mabel only rejoined: "Oh, yes; you want me to go back. I know you want me to give up my own pleasure and go back to Newbould. I tell you I will *not* go."

"Mabel! I do not; *indeed* I do not want you to go *there;* but I can't—I can't explain *here.* Mabel," she cried, in a painful agitation, "listen to me; if you still wish to go by to-morrow's steamer, I will not for a moment hinder you."

"Where would you take me now?" said Mabel, still angrily.

Forcing a more cheerful tone, Ella said: "Only to the hotel over there, just for to-night. Oh, Mabel, for my sake, *do* come!" To this Mabel consented rather peevishly.

Mr. Collingwood, who had now joined them on the wharf, promised to go with the maid to claim the luggage, and to see that all was taken to the hotel, and would then come and meet them there; but Mabel lingered as if to delay fulfilling her promise to come with Ella; she would insist on going personally to aid the search for the luggage, and so it happened that the whole party reached the hotel together.

In vain Ella urged Mabel to take some refreshment, although

she knew from the maid that they had had no meal since breakfast. Mabel was far too impatient to hear this mysterious piece of news which had brought her prudent sister all the way from London to meet her.

Ella began by admitting, in answer to questions, that it was a telegram from Ruth that induced her to take the step of stopping Mabel on her way to the Continent.

She listened sullenly and silent. Then she interrupted suddenly, "I see, I see!" speaking with a strange fierceness, "you want me to go back! It is all a trick—it's Ruth's meddling." Then in a tone that was almost a shout, "I tell you I won't go back to Newbould. No! not even as near as Woodleigh. Don't try to persuade me! I tell you I won't go back—and if John doesn't like it—he—"

"Mabel! Mabel!" cried Ella, breaking through the rush of angry words, "you don't know—*you don't know*, dear; your husband has been very ill—very ill. Mabel!" she said sharply and suddenly, for she saw the angry fierceness was unsubdued, "Mabel!" then more gently, "he is dying, he—is—dead!" and the words fell slowly from Ella's lips, gently becoming more tenderly impressive, as she went on to the last solemn word.

But scarcely had that word been uttered when her startled horror was aroused, a wild cry burst from Mabel, and then, with the wild stare as of a maddened animal, she shrieked, again and again, "Dead! dead!! dead!!!—and I murdered him! Ah!" she cried turning to Ella with an angry scowl, "ah! yes!—yes, you know it. *You* are helping the police—you know they are on my track, yes—ah, ah, ah!" she laughed in a frantic ecstasy of excitement. "Yes! I murdered him—dead! dead!—I shall be hanged!" and she laughed that fearful laugh again.

Ella's horror and dread were too terrible to picture forth; she looked aghast at the madly excited woman, who was shrieking in real agony of mind.

At length, exhausted by her own fury, Mabel sank unconscious on the floor. The frightened maid-servant helped Ella to raise the motionless frame, loosen her dress, and place a pillow under her head. With great thankfulness Ella saw, what she had not before noticed in the hurry and darkness, that the maid was a girl from Woodleigh, whom she had known for years as thoroughly good, trustworthy, and affectionate.

Ella now whispered to Fanny the instructions to find Mr. Collingwood, and to "tell him Mrs. Brownlow is very ill, and bid him come to me in the next room." The girl slipped away and quickly executed the commission; then when Ella heard the advancing steps of her young friend, she motioned to Fanny to take her place in watching Mabel, who was still quite unconscious.

She then went to Mr. Collingwood, told him briefly what had happened, and said she feared for her sister's life and reason unless medical aid were immediately summoned. She owned that she feared if the frenzy should again seize on Mabel the effect would be fatal.

Mr. Collingwood started off at once, and ere long returned with a doctor, and left them, saying he would remain close at hand in his own rooms, to be ready to help in any case of need.

All this time Mabel remained unconscious; the laboured, slow breathing alone gave proof that she was alive; and as Ella sat watching, it seemed as if that heavy stupor must suddenly end life.

The doctor was a kind, cheery old gentleman, and soon made himself acquainted with all details. Ella told him that her sister had started for a trip on the Continent—not, she owned, with her husband's full sanction, but with no fault that the world could blame; told him how, in consequence of the telegram, she had stopped the departure, and that the news of her husband's sudden death had unnerved Mrs. Brownlow, and that she had been like one gone mad, frantically accusing herself of having caused his death.

"I see! I see!" said the good, kind man. Then, after carefully observing his patient, he gave directions that Ella and the maid should undress her, and get her into bed.

Mabel was now apparently conscious, but passive and silent. The doctor would see her again, and prescribe.

They had little difficulty in persuading Mabel to go to bed; she seemed like one walking in sleep. They were hopeful this calm would last, but it was only for a moment. The instant she laid her head on the pillow she started up, and a fresh outburst of the frenzied passion began. It was terrible to witness. Such real terror; then anger; then that cruel shuddering dread, with cries sometimes of rage; then piteous entreaties for help.

Dr. F—— observed the scene for a few moments in patient calmness, listened to the cries, as Mabel uttered with shrieks the dreadful words:

"I murdered him! I poisoned him! Ah, ah! the police are coming!"

Then, while listening and observing all, Dr. F—— poured into the glass, which he had desired to be placed in the room before he entered, a small quantity of liquid from a bottle he had brought with him, all without the least sign of hurry or anxiety.

Marvellous seemed that quiet manner and calmness to Ella's excited heart, but it was soothing, and the certainty of help at hand relieved the distressing strain of her feelings.

Dr. F—— filled up the little glass with water. Then in a very clear and almost cheerful voice the worthy doctor said: "Coming, are they? *Let them come!*" Then slowly and very distinctly, "Do you suppose I should let them interfere with one of MY patients!"

Mabel turned and looked at him, but the poor eyes were the wandering eyes of a maniac, then said plaintively, "Will you be my friend, then? Will *you* help me to escape?"

"MOST CERTAINLY," he replied, very quietly; then added, "now listen, my good lady, you must be very quiet, very quiet, indeed, and your sister and I *will* save you. Have no fear,"—he held up his hand to sign to her that she must not speak—"be quite assured, you need not fear, but you must not speak, and you must be obedient. Drink this—hush! not a word."

While he was thus speaking, she mechanically swallowed the draught. It was a strong opiate. Still holding her hand, feeling the fierce struggle of the beating heart in the responding throbbing pulse, he went on talking slowly, not allowing Mabel to interpose a word, but gently hushing her first endeavour to speak. Very quietly he went on in a tone of calm certainty, using sometimes such queerly chosen words and reasons to prove the absolute certainty of safety, that Ella, in spite of her distress, could scarcely repress a smile. Gradually he spoke less, then was silent. The drug began to take effect. Mabel gently sank back on her pillow. All was quiet. Oh, strange and blessed calm. Those terrible words of the agonised outcries still echoed in the ears of the bystanders; but she who had been so recently in the rage of delirium was now at rest. Only her quiet, regular breathing broke the death-like silence. After a short time Dr. F—— gently withdrew from the bedside, beckoning to Ella to follow into the sitting-room which opened out from the bedroom. He gave her minute directions how to act should any emergency arise, promising to come early next morning; but said he did not anticipate that Mabel would awaken for some hours; if she did, such and such directions were to be carried out, and they might confidently expect she would again fall asleep. He left, and all was quiet.

What an anxious, excited, yet weary time of watching followed. Notwithstanding all the assurances Dr. F—— had given, Ella could not but dread any restlessness in Mabel. And then, notwithstanding the *apparent impossibility*, she had a terror that there were hidden depths that she did not know. Could it be, she asked herself in tremulous horror, that there was some slight foundation of truth in the dreadful words reiterated in that frenzy, "I poisoned him"? There had been such real terror in those words of self-accusation.

The time slowly passed away. Midnight was at length over, then came the cold hours of night—that strange part of our existence generally passed in healthy slumber—in complete oblivion, but it is well known to all who tend the sick and dying, those hours have a peculiar effect on those suffering in a mortal malady. The thread of earthly life is more often snapped during the "small hours" which last two or three hours after midnight than at any other period of the twenty-four.

Towards five o'clock the sleeper moved, and seemed on the point of waking; the medical rules were faithfully carried out, and again Mabel sank into profound slumber, seemingly more peaceful than before.

Soon after her hurried breakfast, during which the kind and zealous Fanny watched, thus permitting Ella the quiet solitude which she sorely needed to recruit her nervous powers, the post brought the promised letter from Ruth.

CHAPTER V

MABEL was sleeping quietly, so Ella was able to study Ruth's letter at leisure. It was long, tenderly kind, but concise. There was much to tell and explain. It was certain that Mr. and Mrs. Brownlow had lately lived unhappily. It was rumoured that there had been constant disagreements. They said that Mr. Brownlow looked ill and harassed, and report said that Mrs. Brownlow seemed to take every opportunity to thwart his wishes and annoy him. This miserable state of matters had been going on for a long while.

The day before Mrs. Brownlow had started for the Continent there had been a serious dispute; it was naïvely added that when Mrs. Brownlow was "put about" all the household very soon knew it.

People said that, in the hearing of the man-servant who was bringing in breakfast, Mrs. Brownlow had announced to her husband that she had *now* fixed to go for her foreign tour. She laughed, and said all was ready, trunks all packed, and that she intended to start the next morning, and then proceed from London.

Mr. Brownlow at first seemed not to treat this seriously, but when he found it was only too real, he tried to induce his wife to postpone her intention.

He said, if she would give up this hasty plan, he would arrange to take her to Paris, and from thence they would visit other places. He spoke very kindly, and said he should enjoy the trip; it might do his health good, he thought. He looked, the man said, very ill, and somewhat distressed. Mrs. Brownlow seemed to listen; then said, "Mind, you are to shut up Newbould, for I mean to stay quite two years." To this Mr. Brownlow refused consent.

He, as far as they could judge, seemed to have been kind and quiet in his manner, but when he refused to shut up the Grange and dismiss the servants, the lady grew very angry. She was distinctly heard to say, as she stood by the open door as she left the room, in what seemed an overpowering passion, "Yes, I will go to-morrow, and more than that, I'll not come here again in a hurry . . . . I don't care what the 'world,' as you call it, will say! I *will* enjoy myself . . . . Oh, yes, I daresay you would not have given me that money I asked for yesterday, if you had known. There, you may enjoy yourself, too." She laughed a bitter, cruel laugh. "You know we hate each other. Yes, *we* do!" she cried shrilly, "and I don't care if I never see you again," and banged the door.

She took her meals in her own room, and, as far as they knew, did not see her husband again that day.

Mr. Brownlow had remained in the library all day, except for meals. When he found his wife did not appear, he asked with his usual thoughtful care what had been sent up to her. The maid said she had gone upstairs twice in the day to seek her, but without success, for the kept her door locked.

He sat up all the night. When the carriage drew up early in the morning to fetch the lady, Mrs. Brownlow went out, and as she passed him, he said, in his usual frank, cheery voice: "Good-bye, Mabel! be sure to write often!"

She just turned her head, and answered simply with "Good-bye," and was gone.

Towards evening Mr. Brownlow seemed really ill. He asked for some coffee to be brought him in the library. He spoke cheerfully. It was evident he was resolved there should be no ground for gossip,—spoke of wind and weather as to Mrs. Brownlow's journey.

When Thomas brought the coffee, he was sure his master was really ill and in pain. The man who had been with him for more than twenty years took courage to ask if he might not send for the doctor. Receiving a refusal, Thomas ventured to say that Miss Brownlow would be vexed if nobody let her know that her brother was unwell; might he send the groom over to the Rectory with a message, asking Miss Ruth to come? "I am sure you are very poorly, sir; Miss Ruth would be very glad to come and stay a bit."

The suggestion was not taken amiss. He replied that it was true he felt ill. It was the old pain he had often had before. He said that if not better in the morning he would send to the doctor, and write and ask Miss Brownlow to come and nurse him. He added, "I am used to this pain; it is not serious. I will go to bed."

Thomas assisted him as usual. Then, before lying down, Mr. Brownlow took his place at the table in his dressing-room, on which were a few papers and books, mostly of a devotional character.

He leaned back in his chair, looking very pale, and rather breathless . . . . Just as Thomas was leaving the room, his master called him back, and speaking with apparently a great effort, said:

"Thomas, you have always been a true and faithful man; you are a friend to me and my family. Don't let any gossip spread; don't allow anybody to speak about your mistress in any way but with the greatest respect. Now listen exactly to what I am going to say . . . . There is no matter of fault, nor any harm whatever, in her going abroad. I should, indeed, have preferred her putting off the journey for a time, for I *cannot* go with her *now*, but perhaps I shall join her. I greatly hope she will enjoy the trip; when she returns she will have plenty to tell, but I think she will soon be tired of foreign ways . . . . Now, *remember* there is *no harm whatever* in her going. I will have no gossip made about it."

Thomas promised he would "speak out," that he would stop any talk if it began, that he should say his master quite approved Mrs. Brownlow's having the little change.

About half an hour later the bell rang. When Thomas answered the summons, Mr. Brownlow was already in bed. He complained of feeling restless, and feared he should not sleep. The man asked if he were in pain. Mr. Brownlow said it was less sudden than usual; if only he could sleep he should be quite right again. He then gave Thomas a key and bade him reach down from the upper shelf of a press that stood in the corner of the room, for a dark blue bottle marked "Sleeping Draught," and told him to place it and a glass within reach of the bed, saying he should not take the medicine unless the pain quite prevented sleep. The man said that his master seemed much surprised that the bottle was not in the place indicated, and asked if anybody had been ill in the house—had there been any searching for medicine?

"No, sir," the man replied, "only you and mistress have a key to this cupboard."

"So I thought," replied Mr. Brownlow, who seemed so confident that the bottle was there, that he arose from the bed and went to search for it himself. No, it was not there!

While searching, Thomas espied on another shelf what looked like the bottle in question. It proved he was right. Mr. Brownlow examined it closely and smelt its contents. The bottle was quite full. He said it was all right, but was puzzled to think how it could be that it had not been left in its proper place. However, he told Thomas to pour out a dose into the medicine-glass, to cover it, and place it within easy reach. He bade Thomas good-night, and all was quiet.

* * * * * * *

In the morning the bell did not ring as usual. Mr. Brownlow was a very early riser. Remembering that the sleeping-draught had probably been taken, Thomas was not uneasy, but at last it was past ten, so he knocked at the door gently, feeling rather anxious. No response. He knocked again more loudly, with no result. He was now alarmed, and with an undefined sense of dread entered the room, and found to his horror his good, kind master "looking just like a corpse," and, touching the hand, knew that his fears were true. The doctor was hurriedly summoned, and confirmed the fact that poor John Brownlow was dead. Probably some hours had elapsed since he passed away from this life in his sleep. The doctor said he had no doubt the cause was heart disease.

The sad story spread rapidly, and as the details of the search for the missing bottle became known, more and more additions gathered round the facts, thus the tidings of the death reached Ruth at the Rectory in *this* terrible form:—

"Mrs. Brownlow had had a dreadful quarrel with her husband, had poisoned him, and gone off to France to escape from justice."

This horrible story was suddenly repeated to Mrs. Graham, with the full weight of the gathered-up inventions. The frightful shock had caused a stroke of paralysis, and she was now lying in a critical state at Woodleigh.

As Ella read on, she learned, however, that Ruth had seen the doctor, and had learned from his own lips that he had no doubt whatever that Mr. Brownlow had died a natural death, and that the horrible rumours were without foundation. He had known for some time past that his patient had serious organic disease of the heart; but he did think that the sorrow, excitement, and grief he had lately endured had increased the mischief, and had been the immediate cause of death taking place at that time. The doctor said that since the unhappy state of home life at the Grange was not unknown, and reports had by this time become greatly exaggerated, it would probably be necessary to hold an inquest, when he felt convinced the verdict after the *post-mortem* examination would set at rest all these rumours. He, therefore, desired Ruth to send the telegram to Ella, as the best means of stopping Mrs. Brownlow's departure, which, under the circumstances, must be done, and as quickly as possible. Ruth had received Ella's telegram, and knew that she and Mabel were together at Harwich, and felt sure she would write soon as she could to set their anxiety at rest.

* * * * * * *

Mabel was still sleeping. Ella, as she read and reread the letter, could do nothing. She could only *wait*, with the heavy burden on her heart. What could it all mean? for Mabel's horrible cry of self-accusation still echoed on her ear. Could there be any real *ground* for that cry, for that terror? Oh! what if the inquest *should* reveal traces of poison? The thought was too dreadful. No! it was, it could only have been the delirium of transient insanity that had forced those cries from poor Mabel.

She could not even venture to arouse the sleeper, and snatch some comfort from a calmed mind on the refreshed awakening.

No! Ella must *wait* . . . .

How much of our life is passed in simply waiting! We long to act, but we must wait; wait for tidings, wait for change, for the hoped-for recovery! or for the death which will darken our lives!

A precious life is in danger! We can only *wait.*

The day passed, and yet another. The doctor was satisfied, for Mabel's calm of unconsciousness was now followed by that quiet natural sleep which is the "best medicine." As yet Ella had not spoken to Mabel, for by the advice of Dr. F——, she had not even entered the bedroom, but remained in the adjoining apartment, the invalid being watched by Fanny, who from time to time reported to Ella the condition of her sister.

Then came a telegram, and the load was once more removed from Ella's heart, as she read that the verdict at the inquest was "death from heart disease." But when the post brought full account of all that had passed during the inquiry, much distress returned. Many strange and unexpected details had been brought forward, as well as the story of the search for the bottle of sleeping mixture, which was fully entered into. Then a chemist who had but recently settled in the vicinity, gave evidence to the effect that Mrs. Brownlow had asked him to supply her with a strong opiate, but that as she was a stranger to him he refused to do so without a doctor's prescription.

Then it appeared that she went to Messrs. Griffin & Sons, the old-established chemists of the nearest town. There she was well known. She made a similar request to old Mr. Griffin, who happened to be in the shop. She asked him to give her "a *very strong* sleeping mixture."

Dates from their diaries proved this was two days after her visit to the stranger chemist.

Mr. Griffin said the lady looked excited; said she had dreadful toothache, and must have something "*very strong*."

The assistant in the shop was a new employé, and was eagerly listening, whereupon old Mr. Griffin, with a loyal feeling to the Brownlow family, abruptly sent the youth out with a somewhat complicated message to the bank, purposely made lengthy that the lady might not be too closely observed.

Mr. Griffin then himself prepared a mixture of a safe but soothing and calming medicine. His opinion then, as now, was that

Mrs. Brownlow was nervous and excited, and that what would benefit her would be *any sort* of medicine which she would believe to be *potent* in its effect! The faith in the efficacy of the drugs would probably be quite sufficient. He, therefore, gave her the bottle gravely, with very minute instructions as to care in taking the "sleeping draught."

Mrs. Brownlow asked whether if "by accident" she took too much it would do her real harm.

To this he evasively replied, "You can never be too careful in taking medicines of this character," and added that she must note the directions.

Mrs. Brownlow took it, paid for it, and left the shop.

Mr. Griffin added that he had told her he would send it with the soda water and some trifles which were just being packed to go to her house, but she said hurriedly, "Oh, no!" and added, as she turned away, "You needn't tell anybody I have this medicine."

The contents of the bottle found by Mr. Brownlow's bedside had been analysed, and proved to be a harmless ordinary calming medicine, and had anyone taken the whole it could not have caused death. The result, too, of the *post-mortem* examination proved that there were no traces of any poison, or, indeed, of any drug, and the state of the heart left no doubt as to the cause of death. The verdict, therefore, was in accordance with the medical report.

Ella waited still, but with a lightened heart, watching by Mabel's bedside.

Soon she awoke fully, and began to speak softly and naturally, but when her sister replied, the vague, wandering expression came back in the eyes—that look of terror which had preceded the previous attacks of frenzy, but Ella said immediately with a forced smile, "All is quite well, dear! There is nothing to make you anxious.

All is *quite well!* I will tell you all about it when you have had your breakfast!" Mabel was about to reply, but her sister instantly arrested the unuttered words. "No! Not one word! Take your breakfast now; then I will come and tell you all my *good* news. Just *believe my word* that all is right!" and quickly left the room. In due time she told Mabel the substance of what had passed, omitting of course, all the details and rumours of suspicions afloat.

Before she told anything circumstantially, she said calmly, "The death was from heart disease only. John did not take *any* of the sleeping draught." A violent sobbing and burst of tears showed at what severe tension poor Mabel's nerves had been strained. After the relief of copious tears she was calmer, and then in somewhat incoherent sentences began again to accuse herself.

Ella gathered that she really *had* entertained the dreadful wish that John might take an overdose of the sleeping mixture, which she knew he used occasionally; that she *did* go and obtain a "*very strong opiate*" from Messrs. Griffin, and had poured it into the dark blue bottle, *instead* of the contents, which she threw away, believing it was *very strong*, and thinking John would some day take a dose of it, and not wake up again!

"Ella," she cried, "I think I was mad! Do you think I was mad or wicked?" While Ella was endeavouring to frame a reply, in uncertainty which was the least terrible alternative to utter, Mabel cried fiercely, "*Answer me!* Was I mad or wicked?—which?"

Quietly, and with loving tact, Ella soothed the excitement. The calm discretion of her words took good effect, and the dreadful excitement passed away without being followed by the frenzy of previous attacks.

After a short time Dr. F—— advised that his patient should be removed into more suitable surroundings, but said if possible she must be kept from scenes where the memory of her recent distress was likely to be once more aroused, advising Ella that the greatest caution must be observed in the choice of their destination.

Mabel continued very quiet, and watched at first the preparations for departure very unconcernedly, but when she became aware that they were going to remove, she roused herself and firmly refused to go back to the Grange. She never actually named Newbould, but would say over and over from time to time, "No, not THERE—not to THAT place! never! never!"

Her growing excitement alarmed Ella, so she answered in a quietly decided tone—"Mabel, but surely you will like to come with me, to dear Woodleigh?"

"Oh, yes, yes, yes!" cried poor Mabel. "Ah! we were so happy there before any of these things happened. Yes, we will go to Woodleigh," and dropping her voice to a tone of plaintive entreaty— "It will be just the same as it was before, won't it?"

Mabel seemed perfectly indifferent when told of her mother's seizure and continued helplessness. Only *once* she said gravely and kindly, "You know, Ella, Mrs. Graham is not *my* mother, she is *yours*, so of course you care for her, and I am sorry you are anxious, but of course her being ill is nothing to *me*."

This was a fixed idea; and it seemed at first wiser not to *combat* it, while of course Ella did not encourage the idea, but always spoke of Mrs. Graham to Mabel as "your mother." Sometimes she was contradicted bluntly, but not with ill-temper; more often Mabel appeared as if she did not hear the words, or as if their meaning did not reach her.

Mabel was very quiet—asked, as she entered the carriage on the morning of departure, where they were going, and on being told they were all to live at Woodleigh again, she smiled the sweet smile of her early days, but did not speak again on the subject.

The journey was safely accomplished; but we must go back a little to explain more fully.

CHAPTER VI

ELLA was, indeed, very desirous of returning to Woodleigh. She was anxious to see Mrs. Graham, having always entertained a measure of affection for the bright, cheerful little lady, and it was a real grief to know that she was now a helpless invalid. The paralytic stroke brought on by the shock of recent events had deprived her of all muscular power, but her mind and memory were quite unimpaired. Mrs. Graham herself heard with extreme satisfaction that Ella and Mabel were coming back to Woodleigh. Full directions for preparing their rooms were sent on. Ella had desired that her own bedroom should be prepared for herself as formerly, and that Mabel's room should be arranged in every way as much as possible according to her taste in olden times.

There was, indeed, joy in the household. To prepare to welcome "our dear Miss Ella" was a work of love. Even the usually taciturn old gardener called to the housemaid, and, when he had secured her attention, delivered the longest speech he had ever been known to utter at one time. "She's going to have her old room again, is Miss Ella. Well! then just you go upstairs and look out at her window while I cut at some of these trees, and you call out and tell me when you can quite well see the graveyard and *that white stone*. Miss Ella will look out of the window the first thing for THAT, I know."

The gardener foretold aright!

But we must be brief.

The journey was safely accomplished. Mabel was in a quiet, absent, dreamy mood, and quite silent. She appeared to be without feeling or emotion of any kind.

. . . . Poor Mrs Graham! What a terrible calamity had fallen on her! All the former bright vivacity had faded away. The burden of helplessness was very sore to her who had always been first and foremost in every matter. Always an early riser, but *now* must wait till others rise; always active to help herself and everybody around her, now dependent, helpless! How sadly changed!

After a while, Ella was delighted to be able to make many arrangements to alleviate the bitterness of the trial, and to give the sufferer a little more of the blessed sense of freedom; but yet, when all was done, the burden of helpless inactivity remained.

But the sharpest pain, almost agony, arose from the change in Mabel. When she brought her into the room where her poor disabled mother was lying, it was sad to see no trace of love, not even a glance of kindly sympathy—she did not even speak words of formal courtesy—she was silent, cold, hard, and utterly unmoved. Even when the scorching tears welled up in the poor invalid's eyes, she made no reply to her mother's words, only seemed restless and impatient to leave the room.

Mrs. Graham's heart-broken sorrow was very real—there were no artificial disguises, no feigned expressions; it was genuine bitter grief, and its quiet hopelessness was most painful to witness.

Mabel continued for some weeks in this cold, dull, impassive state. Ere long there came a gradual change . . . . Alas! there was now no doubt—she was insane. Either the brain had not been able to sustain the shocks caused by her own wilful excitement in the past, or the wild passion which had wrought that excitement had its root in some disease or affection of the brain itself; "Very possibly hereditary," said the doctors.

Ella secured, by their advice, the careful attendance of a skilled companion for Mabel, and was thus relieved from the anxiety of watching her, and enabled to devote herself to the effort of rendering her poor sister as happy as her sad state would permit.

It was now a time of great trial for Ella, for very soon after her return to Woodleigh Mrs. Graham grew rapidly worse, and the fatal close of her malady was not far distant.

She became wonderfully changed; a *real* tenderness in her manner and feelings took the place of the old falseness and insincerity; the former artificial tones, so winning, but so often assumed to hide indifference, had all dropped away.

May we not believe this arose from a deeper self-knowledge? She had never been so simple, so natural before, and thus, without seeking to win it, she found a warm place in Ella's affections, and the tie, which had been a mere form hitherto, became real.

There came a bright spring afternoon. Mrs. Graham's couch had been wheeled close to the open window, and she could thus enjoy the beautiful view beyond the immediate surroundings of the house and picturesque garden. All spoke of coming summer, coming gladness, for birds were gaily singing, and the flowers were bright; all the air was fragrant and full of that promise of "good things to come," which is one of the soul-stirring charms of spring-time.

That longing for summer! How naturally it rises in the heart when the first dawn of spring brightens the earth. We say "Summer is coming" with a throb of gladness! Year after year we say the same, though many a cold, dark day will follow—many a snowstorm it may be—but the past has not quenched the glad expectation; we say it still—"Summer will soon be here!"

Instinct of a higher life! YES, there *will* be summer, and none of earth's disappointments *then.*

* * * * * * *

This was specially a "real summer day," though the almanacs called it only spring.

Ella was reading to Mrs. Graham, one of the invalid's greatest pleasures.

At a pause which presently occurred, Mrs. Graham said in a low but impressive voice, "Put away the book now, dear. I want to talk . . . . Oh, Ella!" she continued, "I have a load on my heart. I cannot hope for any rest, any *true* rest, I mean, until I have told you all about it."

Ella drew her low chair nearer to the couch, while Mrs. Graham, speaking quietly and without excitement, but with tones of deepest feeling, sometimes hesitating, then continuing with a visible effort, *told* ALL.

Breathlessly Ella listened; now a bright flush, then a death-like pallor crept over her face; and then her rapidly-changing colour showed how deeply the words struck into her heart, as Mrs. Graham told circumstantially and quietly the tale of her deceitful trick. She made no excuses, but told of the sudden temptation, of the exchanged envelopes, of the forged alteration of the name in the letter, so as to efface the "Ella" which poor John *had* written, and to substitute, by the slight changes she had made, the name of "May" instead. And then, without giving Ella time to speak, Mrs. Graham cried in a voice of real *agony* of heart, "Ella! Ella! is your forgiveness *quite* impossible?"

Softly Ella rose, and, kneeling by the side of the couch, took the cold, helpless hand in hers with a gentle, loving pressure, and said:

"Impossible! Oh, no! *not* impossible; it is given—immediately, and with my whole heart—before you asked me—you were forgiven while you were still speaking. I *do*, I do with my whole heart forgive you! for oh! I am so deeply thankful! oh, *so* thankful that you have told me all, for *now*, NOW there is no bitterness of self-reproach for me, no feeling of humiliation; for, dear Mrs. Graham," continued Ella, "one day John said very loving words, and now I know he DID mean them for *me*; he meant what he said, and I was *not* forward and unwomanly in having taken those words into my heart! ALL *my burden* is gone now, and YOU have comforted me."

From that time, Ella, having taken that deep comfort into her wounded spirit, seemed altogether changed.

She had, indeed, since the time she left Woodleigh, always been busy, and loving, and even cheerful; but she had never had the brightness of her early days.

Now! why, brightness, and joy, and gladness, seemed to be the very air she breathed! and the cheerfulness she diffused around her. Her chief aim was now to soothe and comfort Mrs. Graham, and her tender pity became constantly deeper, though sometimes, *for a few moments*, damped by the sense of utter misery caused to *others* by the cruel deception that had been practised.

A few weeks later, when Ella was sitting near her stepmother, the unhappy woman, after a great effort at self-control, told her that she *knew* there was hereditary insanity in one branch of the family of Mabel's father. In fact, as *even now* she seemed reluctant to own, Archibald Graham himself became insane, and was under the charge of a professional attendant for many months before he died.

She had no hope of improvement in Mabel's condition, and sorrowed bitterly at the knowledge of *her own sin* in the miserable "trick" that had brought calamity on her child, having probably developed into this insanity the seed of the inherited malady.

"Mabel did not care at all for John. I knew it; yet I forced her to accept him. And now!"—hot tears fell as she spoke—"and now, will not all his misery, and her wild temper, and her madness, be charged as a load of sin to *my* account?"

* * * * * * *

It was long ere this terrible depression of remorse became softened to the burdened conscience.

In a light tale like this, it might border on irreverence did one speak or even hint more *fully* of high and holy things; but in closing this sad history of the miserable results of deception and of unresisted temptation, it must be added that at length the agony of remorse became true contrition, and the poor sin-stricken soul was led into the one only sure refuge, and found peace. And after lingering a few months after this happy change, she died peacefully and without pain, Ella always near, and cherishing her with loving care and watchfulness to the end.

* * * * * * *

"Poor little Mabel," as in long-ago days Ella loved to call her, when the girl had got into trouble with her not infrequent youthful scrapes, "Poor little Mabel" lived in comfort for five or six years at Woodleigh. The form which her insanity had now taken was very gentle. It was, in fact, more an increasing weakness of intellect than what is generally known as insanity. There were no outbursts of frenzy, and her gentle manners made her very lovable. She would play like a child with trifles, or with flowers; these she would cherish, and kiss again and again. And sometimes a sweet ringing laugh was heard, so like the merry sounds of her laughter in early girlhood, that tears would come into Ella's eyes when she heard it, and truly none who knew the story could hear that laugh and remain unmoved.

* * * * * * *

When Mabel died, and the sad tale had softened in her memory, Ella had a new interest in life. She had, indeed, been very happy in her quiet country home. All the villagers, far and wide, felt the blessings that flowed directly or indirectly from her influence. But when her time was fully at liberty, after her sister's death, Ruth Brownlow came to share the home, and together they took entire charge of some orphan (and penniless) grandchildren of good old Mr. Reynolds, the rector of the neighbouring parish, who has been already mentioned incidentally in this narrative. So a peaceful life ran its course, and when, at length, Ella was laid in the quiet grave where her own beloved mother had rested for so many years, a crowd of sorrowing folk followed the funeral, joining tearfully, but in deep reverence, with sure and certain hope, in the burial service.

The story is not yet forgotten. Should you visit the neighbourhood of Woodleigh, even now, faces will brighten and eyes will be moist, if you question the villagers and hear them speak about their memory of "Our Miss Ella."

AN AUTHENTIC STORY OF A DOG

AN AUTHENTIC STORY OF A DOG

IT was a bright autumn afternoon, and I stood on my doorstep deliberating as to the direction in which I should turn my steps.

I had no special object in view, but the fresh air made the idea of a walk highly attractive, even though there was no ultimate aim in my intentions.

Which way should I turn? Not down into the dusty town; still less was I in a mood to go and mingle with the motley crowd on the esplanade, for just then, to quote Longfellow's beautiful words: "The sorrows of others threw their shadows over me," and my heart was heavy.[8] To the village of H——, and thence to the grassy hills beyond?

Just so! and I started in that direction. The road led upward, and at first was dull and uninteresting, for it was fenced in on one side by a high wall, and on the other by palings, over which I could only see the outer ridge of the thickly planted shrubbery which surrounds C—— Park.

As I turned from the terrace where I lived into this road, I noticed a dog. Unmistakably a "cur of low degree," he was slinking under the park palings with drooping tail and depressed ears.[9] As soon, however, as he saw me, he suddenly changed his abject demeanour, and came up to me with a brisk trot and a knowing cock of one ear, and *said* (as plainly as any human speech could have

---

[8] Paraphrasing lines from 'The Bridge' by Henry Wadsworth Longfellow: 'And only the sorrow of others/Throws its shadow over me.'

[9] Most likely a reference to *Guy Mannering* by Sir Walter Scott.

expressed it), "You are just the sort of person I want; may I go with you and pretend to be your dog?"

I replied aloud—"Certainly, old fellow, *I* have no objection."

Thereupon he wagged his vulgar tail, and trotted by my side; and, now and then, just as if he had been a lady's pet all his days, ran frolicking on a bit, dashing back to me in a light gambolling canter! looking up at me and dancing before me exactly as some valuable toy-terrier accustomed to be admired might have done.

I spoke to him once or twice, which seemed to please him immensely.

The pretence that he was my dog was so cleverly carried out, that happening to meet a lady who was riving herself in a little pony-carriage, and who stopped to greet me and chat a little, her first exclamation (after the ordinary salutations) was, "But oh! where did you pick up that cur? Surely you do not mean to keep him!"

"I did not pick him up," I replied; "he picked *me* up! You should ask him if he is going to keep me!!"

After this interruption the dog and I walked on for some ten minutes farther. Then, at a slight turn of the road I knew why he wanted to me *my* dog! The road, as I said before, was well fenced in, no escape for a dog to run into for shelter, and some fifty yards off there sat a man breaking stones (and *a boy* with him), and there was consequently a heap of stones, nice little stones, close handy, just the size to throw at a dog!

Now, my poor cur was of that class of dog at whom nearly every boy casts a stone: whether wilfully, in spite, or recklessly, in fun, for the cruel amusement of frightening a poor abject wretch.

My dog friend drew a little nearer to me, and looked up anxiously. "All right, old boy!" I said in a cheery voice, "you are my dog, and I'll take care of you!"

He kept just in front of me, with erect tail and well-set-up ears, looking back over his shoulder now and again, as if he were protecting *me!!* I spoke whenever I met his eye.

We passed the stonebreakers—and then, when we were a full stone's throw beyond them, the dog ran on. I supposed he was only thinking of himself all the time; and began to moralise on ingratitude, and other seemingly appropriate and dreary topics, when my four-legged friend suddenly stopped short, looked back, tipped me a most familiar wink—(I am sorry to use such an expression, but I cannot find any other *suitable* words)—and then went off in a sort of three-legged shambling gallop, and I saw him no more.

Hence I knew: 1st, the dog wanted to go to H——; 2nd, he knew there were stonebreakers on the way; 3rd, he wanted protection; 4th, he knew that a woman would protect him; so you see he asked for protection from me, and he received it.

But the strange part of this true story is this—how did such a very vulgar cur guess how to frolic and amble to and fro, and pretend so cleverly to be a pet dog? That poor cur, after many years, has still a place in the dog-corner in my memory.

THE END

www.ingramcontent.com/pod-product-compliance
Lightning Source LLC
Chambersburg PA
CBHW030613310726
48979CB00003B/698

* 9 7 8 1 9 1 7 1 1 3 1 1 3 *